The Truth

M. Ikbal Harb

The author's writings revolve around the human and social problems that afflict people wherever they are. Everyone is equal in the author's entity as a brother in humanity with its colors, races, ethnicities, and cultures. It also includes the defense of the human rights of a woman and a man, a tortured child and a homeless one, the ignorant and the learned, and the disabled and displaced victims of conflicts and wars. Analyzes reality and explores the future through novels, collections of stories, and articles.

The novel **"Here the seducer lies"** fiercely defends the female and explains the inherited customs and traditions and the tribal pimples that ravage her and deprive her of her rights and freedom as a human being.

The Holy Cursed is a philosophical novel that explores the eternal struggle between good and evil and the depth of the relationship between man and the universe.

The last novel, **"The Oracle with the Black Beak,"** recounts and chronicles a century, with the symbolism of its heroes, the chicken kingdoms, of events that affected many countries worldwide. It can be seen as the second part of **"Telling the Truth."**

The collection of stories, **"Long Live the Order,"** analyzes and refutes the types of terrorism, in society, at home, and in terrorist organizations through stories based on the human truth everywhere.

The other world inspired the **"New Blind"** collection of stories as a dimension parallel to our planet. Full of imagination and surprises through proposals and future problems on different levels.

The poetic collective **"The Lover of Oblivion"** is a sentimental group described by the *Italian poet Mario Ragli* as a model of Pablo Neruda's work.

The **"Birth of a Poet"** collection, published in English and Italian, is a collection of translated excerpts from The Lover of Oblivion.

"Death of a Poet" is a collection of stories about the suffering and misery of a poor person in a society that knows animal rights and turns away from human rights.

The importance of the author's works, which are primarily fictional and symbolic, do not talk about a specific place or specific characters. The tear of joy is the same for all people as the tear of sadness, and the descriptions of racism and tyranny are the same anywhere on the planet. Reading reality and diving into human feelings inspires him to discover the future of humanity and spread the truth hidden from many people. Writing about the Earth's relationship with the universe is a constant obsession in the author's writings.

DEDICATION

To the lady of munificence,

To my muse,

To the one in whose eyes I read the truth.

CONTENTS

Praise for "The Truth"

"The writer Mohammad Ikbal Harb did justice to the truth by choosing it as title for his novel to lead us trough it to an entrance that would take us to a space of reality on which the writer sheds light by unveiling the truth's face and evealing of it what - he thinks - is its true face. He wove its parts skillfully and formed of it a literary subject, thus turning it into a creative composition and a useful invention that would provide receivers with a perception and an interpretation which result in elevation. It would also inspire them to polish the taste and hone human reaction that might lead, in its turn, to kindness away from harsh interaction and rude confrontation with every truth that differs from our familiarities and contradicts our expectations and assumptions."

—Rayid Mahdi (Iraq)

"The writer brought the past and the present together through his writing style giving significance back to conventional story in the first place while keeping old literary language within a modern frame that varied between symbolism and directness at the level of style according to the reality."

—Morad Yousoufi

"Narration wove between them a love story regardless of their different way of life as each of them perceived the world differently as well as their ways of settling in the universe...[A]fter a love story that brought them together, narrative fates parted them with the help of his chicken species."

—Fawzi Dimasi (Tunisia)

The Beginning of a Whisper

10

In their last days, the dangling grape vines looked like the legs of an old woman hiding behind time curtain with a memory yearning for a bygone youth. Then she would steal photos from freshness memory that left its remnants in the museum of fate unlike grapes which started to regain their vigor in the golden jars in the aftermath of a fadedness that was almost on the brink of death and changed into a drink the colors of which were vacillating between gold and crimson, the most precious thing that son of Adam has ever possessed.

A drink that would impart a fake happiness about a delusive youth to anyone whose dreams died, while they are still alive and would derange anyone who was worn out by their mind that they would be content with little even if it is a delusion.

At the roots of one of the grape vines, a fully-grown rooster was perching up here and there dallying with nature. He was delighted with windfall grapes that son of Adam abstained from collecting. He pecked at this and smashed that for his chicks. He played with them, and jumped among them, sometimes to make them laugh, sometimes to teach them. And though he loved his kids and spent quality of time having fun together, his behavior was not void of male vanity as well as the pride of the governor because there were among his kids a lot of males that would rule after him and would even help him with expanding his sovereignty over other farms.

On the pergola that was covering the sky of that bunch of chickens; a migrating little bird was frolicking. She adorned with her colors the pergola's as if she was an emerald on a golden bed consisting of the yellowish leaves of the grape vine arbor. It was her first immigration with her own kind. She was driven by love for exploration and yearning for knowledge. For this reason, she found pleasure and comfort at every stop after traveling tiredness.

The former travelers told her that she would find a different place here. She would find nature in the bosom of the valley, a hill on the clouds with an abundance of water and pasture and feel the breeze of son of Adam's civilization through ages. They told her that affection and glory, cruelty and spite, creativity and sublimity, construction and destruction would provoke her thinking. They told her that great men, whose price was paid by many innocent people and those who were not, passed by here

It was an incomparable place the most beautiful about it was that son of Adam left a civilization made of stone for nature; hence, it drew the most wonderful picture of time. But he would sometimes come back to practice the sport of killing against others, and that's why she had to be careful of this monster that claimed once to be God. She mastered dealing with nature and its creatures. Here she was playing with birds and chasing tiny insects. And whenever ravenous birds disquieted her , she would escape out of fright from the big to frighten the small...she did all this happily as if she knew deep down that she might not reach her destination and if she did, her hope of homecoming would be slimmer. Her distress would not change anything as she instinctively realized this truth. For this reason, she was singing, dancing and flying where she was destined to go during winter journey.

While she was chasing a beetle looking for a supply for winter pantry, a stray gunshot hit her and frightened her out of her wits. She sank in the space and fell on the ground, a body floating in the midst of pains of the wound and horror of the accident.

2

She opened her little eyelids to welcome a new morning, or rather a new era that she didn't take into her consideration...and how would she being a creature that lived from day to day? She used to look at the vast horizon and see clouds with new different shapes. They were permeated with holes that let sunbeam with its numerous colors pass through, bringing along with it the sweetness of the far universe mingled with the delicacy of the feelings of stars in the Milky Way.

She knew innately that every color was a mixture of the moment, an amalgamation of substance, feelings and reflections of every living thing and inanimate object surrounding her. Every single moment had its own unique unrepeatable feeling. And any tenderness that she didn't sense was a loss which cannot be retrieved. Also, she realized that when time once gone, would never come back. For this reason, she accepted the invitation to life. She woke up with a passion for

life rushing into every single cell of her body. But...
the sky was no longer what it used to be. Neither
were clouds. The sky was so close and it was made
of straw and there were two strange eyes looking at
her, one on the right side, and the other on the left
side. Strange eyes and a sky she was not familiar
with.

"O my God!" she trilled these words and then
unconsciously decided to fly out. "Ouch, ouch!" she
said in a painful voice. She looked astonished
rather than scared. Everything was new. It was a
different world.

What's this bed or rather what are these eyes?
Oh my God! What happened to the freedom to
move and fly?

She was humiliated which made her
feel broken. Her eyes were filled with a running
brook of remorse tears, then the sea in them
overflowed and a flood of sorrow began.

"Don't panic," said the creature with bulging
eye on her right-hand side. "You are safe," he
added.

"How can I not panic when I am held hostage
in this strange place added to the fact that I cannot
fly. Are you the hunters I was told about?"

"No, of course not. I'm the doctor of chickens
and this is Sahm, the great rooster, the farm
governor. You were hit by a gunshot yesterday and
blacked out. Then Sahm had brought you here
before the hunter would take you and kill you to

make you into a delicious dish. Next, he called on me to treat your wounds," the other creature answered.

"Oh my God! Is my injury serious?"

"Yes. You must rest here for a period of time that might last long till your wound heals and you can fly again," the doctor said.

"What? A long period..." She looked right and left and her eye met with that of Sahm. "Please, carry me and fly to the gathering place for my flock. Birds will look after me during their traveling," she told him.

"I beg your forgiveness, darling, I can't do that for their place is far and high and I cannot fly," Sahm answered her.

She looked at them repeatedly with scrutinizing eyes. "I felt somewhat comfortable with you, but now doubt starts to overcome me again. Why can't you fly? You have feathered wings, a beak and a tail? You possess what I possess though you're much bigger which means you're more capable of flying than me."

"No, it's not like that at all. We belong to the world of chickens and chickens cannot fly," Sahm answered her.

Silence reigned in the place as if a hunter hovered around it. Sad, the bird closed her lashes.

Oh, how couldn't I pay attention to her saying 'doctor of chickens'? O woe is me! These two are of

15

the underprivileged that our ancestors told us
about. No one of us has met them since long time.
Oh my God! How would I trust them to heal me?
They should treat their lesions first. Oh, how tired
I am! Or rather how hungry and thirsty I am!

Her train of thought was soon interrupted by
the doctor who said, "You should get some rest.
Don't be sad because sadness would delay healing
and speed up misery."

"Please, leave me alone. I'm undergoing a
double sorrow and my worry is bigger than this
news that sometimes tossed me and fell on me at
other times," the bird said.

"What do you mean by double sorrow or
rather what's your name? Can't you see that you
haven't told us your name yet?" Sahm said.

"My name is Awtar. I beg you to forget what I
had told you, especially that I can't accept help
from the underprivileged," she answered.

"Your name bears melodies within it," Sahm
said.

"Who told you that we are underprivileged?
We are well off, or rather very rich," the doctor
said.

"That's not my point. Nevertheless, leave me
alone. I have to leave in a few minutes," Awtar said.

"I'm not going to blame you because you are
sick. Please do not be reckless for you are wounded
and recovery might take a few weeks. Still, you

won't be able to fly because the wound is deep between the body and the wing; hence, your flock should wait," answered the doctor.

"Waiting?! Ah ah, the flock will not wait for me. Sickness is merciless and my staying here is but stressful and boring. Let me leave before it's too late. I beg you," Awtar answered.

Sahm gave her a tender and affectionate look. "Is it reasonable that they would leave such a delicate and sweet bird in trouble and pain and travel away?" he asked. "I will call one of the hens to look after you."

"Don't," she said that with tears swinging in her eyes. "We, aerial birds, put the future of the group before individual interest. We do not wait for those who couldn't catch up with the flock or are wounded. We must reach our destination at the scheduled time to lay eggs before climate starts to change because life journey has to carry on in spite of hurdles and pains. Also, we do not accept any help from you. "

"What are you saying? Your way of speaking shows a lot of derision. You are an aerial bird and I'm a terrestrial one. I don't know what is weird about that, or rather I don't get your point. Or is it my reward because I helped you and disregarded my wives' feelings by spending the whole previous night with you?" he said.

"Really, I'm deeply indebted to you and I wish you would not take it personal. There is no time for discussion. Also, we, species of aerial birds have been traveling at scheduled time since thousands of years. We cross thousand miles and some of us would die from exhaustion or shooting or predation and even from scarcity of food at some stages. We have many enemies; hence, we don't have time to wait or grieve. The new generation is coming in spite of everything. The journey of life doesn't stop for the sake of any creature," she said.

"I'm still unable to understand your lifestyle. I'm so busy and I've never thought of traveling for I have always waited for my chickens to lay eggs or hatch for days, or rather weeks. I live to look after my family and my farm. I don't have time to travel," he said.

"How could such a rooster that has never left this spot realize the importance of time? The world is bigger than this hill. How stupid you are! Though it seems that you don't have a lot of work to do, you find excuses to stay in your isolation and your dark world," she said.

Her words hurt him. He swallowed the lump in his throat; he felt that his pride was wounded. He looked at her in astonishment, turned around and walked away.

She is undoubtedly a crazy bird, but she is beautiful and attractive, he thought. If I don't take care of her and put her into a safe place she would face perils that might cause her death. However his gazes and erect crest spoke volumes.

She realized what was going on in his mind and what her situation was like, so she made it right. She said, "I didn't mean any offense. I mean that one cannot judge without trying. O noble rooster, do not worry. You helped me a lot, but there is no time for discussion for the flock started to take shape and I have to go. Pray that I will reach my goal. Goodbye."

He answered, feeling deep pity for her, "Goodbye my beautiful bird. The only birds I have ever seen on earth are my hens that I thought they are the most beautiful of all. Woe is me! There is a world of beauty overwhelming this universe that we haven't discovered yet. How ironic!" he said that with shyness as his crest got redder than it was. "Really, I don't know too much," he added as he watched her getting ready for flying. But her weak body did not respond to her strong will. She rose to a height of a few feet, and then fell down that her scream resounded to fill the bush with sadness. Her fall shook his senses up. He rushed to her driven by a weird feeling that he simply understood as his desire to help her.

The sensation was strange for the world of chickens did not understand these feelings especially roosters that did not lay eggs or hatch, not to mention the fact that they have to look after thousands of chickens.

Why did he have this beautiful feeling for this strange bird? How would he react if his hens find about this horrible deed. He did not think about this at all. Instead, he rushed to her and asked her, "Are you okay?"

"I don't know," she said, "I'm in great pain."

"Please do not scream, because some hunters might take notice of you and then will kill you or catch you," he said.

"Thank you. Though I hurt you with my words, you came back to help me. I wish I could die from embarrassment."

She fell silent for a few seconds, and then burst into tears. "Look over there, the flock left," she added.

"Don't lose hope. Another flock might pass by," he said.

"There is no way that I am going to survive to see another flock."

3

He took her to a safe place as far as possible from his kingdom and asked her not to move till he could find a way that would comfort her and implant in her heart relief and reassurance. "You must get some rest and do not fly for a prolonged period of time," the doctor said firmly as she looked at her with motherly affection and pity that a healthy old man would feel toward a sick youngster.

"It's out of the question," the bird said. "I'm from a faraway country apart from belonging to a different species, she added. "I don't know anyone here and can't impose myself, either. I will try to leave tomorrow even on foot," she said with pride and haughtiness, while her gazes fixed on the rooster betrayed her.

"When this friend came to me panicked, I thought that a disaster fell upon his family because of the worry and panic I saw. To my surprise I see a little bird that has nothing to do with our community," the doctor said.

"I'm sorry, madam. I'm just a passerby and this noble master is soft-hearted toward passersby. He is the master as you said. Isn't he? And masters are always noble and majestic," the bird said.

"Really, you are in the presence of the farm governor and the noblest of all chickens," the doctor said.

"Do not flatter me for one of the hospitality duties of chickens is to treat the guest as a family member," the rooster said.

The doctor was surprised at his words because chickens cared only about themselves and were known for being cowardly. Her astonishment increased when she remembered that he was in charge of hundreds of chickens, but she realized that he liked her.

She said, "I beg you not to move too much and not to fly till you recover." And then she added, "How are you going to catch up with your flock later?

"As for the flock, it will come back here only after a year and I must be where they lost me. They would send patrolling teams looking through the places where the bird was left behind, then. If he is still alive they would find him," she said.

The doctor said, "Indeed, these intelligence and organization are typical of aerial birds." And then she added, "I will see you after two days to check your wound. See you soon."

As the doctor was leaving, the rooster told her in a low voice, "Please do not tell your friends about what you saw. I will take her to a safe place."

"Don't worry. Your secret is safe with me."

The doctor left, but deep in her heart there was hatred toward this bird or rather fear of this one coming from a different world. But she was the rooster's friend, the master and the protector of the region and she promised not to disclose his secret. As for our friend the rooster, he offered her some grape grains that she started to pierce with her small beak while he was looking at her admiringly comparing her with the neighborhood's hens, her cheerful feather colors with theirs which were dull, and her softness with their roughness. As for her, she was looking stealthily at his crest that was rarely found among her species. She respected his pride mingled with responsibility. His compassion toward her affected her immensely. *Is this typical of this underprivileged species?* She wondered.

He took his leave for a few moments till he found a suitable place safe from stray animals and Man. He returned after a while, and carried her on his back to a place he thought to be perfect. He put her in a basil bush. "This is a safe place that provides you with air and light," he said.

"But it is exposed from below," she said.

"I know that. There are a lot of pebbles nearby. I will gather what suffices to build a fence around the basil trunk."

He built the so-called fence and asked her if she liked it. She said it was so good that he could not enter and she could not exit.

"Don't be sad. I made a secret entrance through which I can enter tomorrow when I will bring you food and the things that the doctor requested. Bye. I will see you tomorrow."

4

A few days passed during which he visited her daily more than once. He brought her the best grains that he thought would be the best for her recovery. These rare kinds of grains they stored for fighters if they were wounded in the battlefield. He also brought her small worms on the chickens' doctor's recommendation. He got closer to her and grew fonder of her personality rather than of her feather that she kept clean and shiny as well as her sweet voice that pleased him and teased his heart. As for her, she was recovering slowly. She waited for his coming yearningly because he was the only creature that she saw bringing her what would keep her alive. And from time to time the doctor would come with him.

His hard feather showed a strength that made her feel safe and his crest with tense colors imparted a sort of pride to her for being the master's concubine. His daily presence was the safety valve that kept her heartbeat steady. They talked about her family, her country, her travels, the universe wonders and the cruelty of son of Adam who owned cows to satisfy his gluttony, then did everything in his power to kill little birds that were neither nourishing nor filling.

He started to tell her about his farm and wives, his field and chicks. A long while after, he began to feel comfortable and happy when she was around, so he started to complain about his wives and his kids' needs including shelter, food and protection. And since autumn was approaching the provision would be scarce; hence, nagging would increase. However, winter was his big plight for there was no escape from nagging. She laughed a lot at this complaint that her cheerfulness was more obvious to him than ever before.

There was another facet of life here disturbing hers. It was not just loneliness and living away from home, but also the fact that the rooster belonged to a different species that she learned it was an inferior one, that of the underprivileged. Their history mentioned that the big fight began a thousand years ago before the great event that changed the course of the history of bird world or feathery birds as it used to be known. The event resulted in two bird worlds: one is terrestrial, the other is aerial. And that he had different religious principles affected her for she heard him some time ago crowing as he was coming to her. She asked him about his scream and he told her that he crowed every morning. He explained to her that it was his prayer.

"Do you bother all creatures with a fierce voice and then you call it worship? Fear God, darling!" she said.

"Do you pray?" he said

"Yes, I do in a soft voice at times and places in which I won't bother anyone as the Merciful asked us to do," she said.

"We do the same thing, but our way is different according to our inherited precepts," he said.

"This is nonsense. Our scholars told us that some birds, especially terrestrial ones deviated from the creed and came up with imaginary things just to create differences that they would use to serve their personal interests owned by ordinary ones of their species," she said.

"Our scholars said that this is the best types of glorification of God, whereas your saying about glorifying God in a melodious voice is aberrance, because it is about singing and melancholy," he said.

"The melodious voice is a gift endowed by God and talking about his blessings is a virtue. Also, our scholars said that an acoustic proficiency is a reflection of heart's submissiveness," she said.

"That's impossible! A beautiful voice is known to draw attention and keep the heart away from remembering God," he said.

"That's insane because beauty fills the universe. Does everything beautiful keep you away from God? Beauty is a blessing that urges you to glorify Him more," she said.

"What our scholars said comes from the heart of books. Still, everyone works hard to get closer to God through a way that will guarantee him or her satisfaction," he said.

She said," You can't be right for we possess the origin of books. And our precepts tell us about the main cause of the occurrence of the bird disaster a thousand years ago which led to the partition of our world into two: one is aerial, the other is terrestrial. It's we who are following the right path." And then she added, "Don't get me wrong. I feel so comfortable with you, but the issue of worship matters to me a lot and I won't reject what our scholars said."

"Always villains found an inlet to clauses of worshipping God and built upon it doctrines and legends to rule ordinary people, so that they could make them believe that they are at the core of worship. All doors have two entrances; one is used to bring creatures closer to each other and surmount differences, another is used to ignite the fire of strife thus helping them to achieve their goals.

"I don't think that there is a correct prayer and an incorrect one. Undoubtedly, there are rituals to be followed to maintain the sacredness and spirituality of prayer between the servant and his God, but sometimes these rituals and ceremonies, that people in power enacted, are a rope that is tied around commoners' neck to be at their command. They are putting chains around their necks under the name of God and divide us into groups that all claim to be the closest. Isn't the distance between God and all creatures the same?" he said.

"It is a must to follow scientist and scholars when practicing our rituals," she said.

"Since faith is the means and God's satisfaction is the goal and since submissiveness and praying God in a good heart are hoped for; therefore, the way of this scholar or that worshipper is not the criterion. All worships would ascend to God who will accept whatever he likes."

he said.

He fell silent for a while and then told her, "I must go now. I'll be back and we can talk calmly."

"It's OK. Can I call you 'Sayah', because you crow?" she said.

-"Of course, you can if you let me call you 'Nagham' because of the softness of your voice and your tender feelings," he said.

"You are making me blush, but I liked this name...see you Sayah," she said.

"See you Nagham," he said.

The incident ended peacefully as it had already been mentioned. They decided to talk again. Her name became 'Nagham' and his became 'Sayah'. They dropped the subject for some long time.

5

The next day, after the call to prayer, Sayah completed some conjugal chores and administrative works and then he took some grains and some grapes. He sneaked through the wood for fear that someone would follow him and headed toward where his heart became his guide. On his way, he was taken aback by some young roosters from his farm and nearby ones coming from the way he was heading to.

"Where were you?" he asked. "Shouldn't you be in the company of the first teacher whom the presidency of farms sent to prepare a successful generation of leaders?"

"Yes. This is what happened," they said.

"How is it possible? The school is behind me, while you are in front of me?" he said.

The teacher wanted to educate us on how to deal with nature, but we ended up learning how to punish those who went astray thanks to your son Haffar.

Sahm smiled proudly at his son Haffar and then said to them, "May God bless you. Go home."

He left them and continued his way to visit Nagham.

Who are those who went astray? he wondered. I didn't know that there is a group that went astray and another that is on the right path among birds and animals. Perhaps they mean son of Adam who likes to slaughter us and burn us up!!! But how are they going to punish him? Oh my God how are things getting complicated with this generation? Let the teacher do whatever he likes. I'm going to see a beautiful face.

Before reaching the bush, he started to crow trying to beautify his voice that Nagham thought was dissonant. To his surprise, he saw something that frightened him; stones were scattered and colorful feathers were on the ground. He ran, or rather gave little jumps in the hope of seeing the surrounding area clearly. He entered the hiding place, but didn't find her. He looked around, but saw nothing but some feathers scattered here and there. Ruby blood drops ignited feelings and flashed in heart that tears of love and sorrow dripped from eyes to slake the parchedness of the situation.

He started to turn over the ground, peck the logs and dig up the grass calling her in a sad voice that had never come from a rooster...but he did not find her. He feared for her.

Did a wolf devour her or did a stray dog eat her? Did son of Adam hunt her! Yes, son of Adam would kill the one that is in good health and finish off the one that is wounded. But foxes are slier and more guileful. But where is she? She was in a safe place for a long time and was on the way to recovery. I could hardly go near her. What happened? Have mercy on me, oh God.

All this was useless, so he looked up at the sky and implored God to be with her wherever she was, be kind to her and bring her back unharmed and healthy. The day was burned and the sun dimmed. The moon sparkled and stars lighted, while he was still digging, pecking and crying. Still, he returned empty-handed. He went out from there carrying a broken heart; a helpless rooster looking for revenge. Her echo and longing sneaked trough the woodwork and exploded streams of tears that flowed into his lake of memories.

He set out for home heartbroken, disheartened and absent-minded. His body returned alone to his dunghill without knowing where he was. He felt asleep though his soul remained in the world of longing wondering whether he should board the ship of memory or burn with waiting at lovers' station.

6

This year, as every year, autumn days passed hard. The leaves of trees fell under the gust of wind, the small twigs were broken and the big ones grieved over them, or rather their biggest grief over hope blossoms in the garden of longing was bigger. Lovers absented themselves from trees' shade and nature refused to let people in love meet and hang around among shady branches.

Nature's sorrow was more violent than Man's grudge and every gust of wind was washing the stuck filth on here and there. And with the fall of every flower, a memory volcano would explode in the heart of a certain lover, a creature somewhere.

The heart of our friend Sayah was shaken. He kept blaming himself. Had he an ounce of power as he claimed, he would have taken her to his hen-house, or rather had he loved her as he claimed, he would have told every living soul about her with pride. He realized that too late, so he kept blaming himself for his cowardice and fear from his hens. But this had been typical of chickens since he came into this world. Could a rooster get rid of his cowardice? That you gave up on your qualities was so hard. He kept going out in the midst of the storm and through the rain. He called her but she didn't answer him!! Sometimes he would send his love, voice, and longing through the wind and at other times through breeze, but there was no answer that would warm a lover's heart. He knew that she was near him somewhere, but he was scared of his delusions. Could she still be alive? Yes. She was alive. That's what his senses were telling him, but his mind was thinking somewhat wisely and prudently.

Winter came on and nothing had changed. Life continued on the farm, on the hill and even in the universe. His night was so long and his days were sad, but life went on as if nothing happened. The era of shrinking started in the world; everything in his eyes was shrinking and vanishing, and in spite of that he didn't find Nagham. He tried to escape her memory, but couldn't. It was hard for him to forget her as he every day saw his hens, such as they were, fat and slow clucking harshly and dissonantly. And whenever he saw a flock of birds in the sky, he would wonder if Nagham was among them. He thought of resorting to a nearby hermitage to share a hermit his seclusion, learn supplication and meditation. He started to look for what would strengthen his bond with God to give him comfort and reassurance.

Along with previous events, he found that life requirements and the responsibility for ruling were keeping him busy apart from providing food and taking care of hundreds of chickens.

One evening as clear as a rooster's eye, Nagham manifested herself with her softness. He smiled at her. He heard sky symphony talking to him secretly and a spectrum of her wings overwhelmed him. He remembered her determination, pride, her capability of fighting as well as her delicacy and tenderness that heightened her beauty. She had what would sharpen her determination and share with him the world of intelligence and power in which he was living. He looked up at the sky imploring God to overwhelm her soul with his mercy.

Clouds roaming in the horizon, then wept, tears of the sky cascaded down from the Milky Way and stars fell down. There was in the sky someone who could feel us and share our sorrows that universes would cry for our unhappiness. His filths were washed by the galaxy's tears, and thus he slept sound after he had seen his beloved's smile at the North Star.

The Secret of the Other Side

In another place on the opposite bank of the life river at the other side of this hill, there were some roosters in a small hole at a mountain summit they called grotto. The place was far from life bustle, in the middle of which there was a little pond formed of gathering of water dripping from a fractured rock ceiling. There were four little roosters and another that witnessed too many winters. This rooster stood to tell them, "Now you realize the reason why you are here or rather you realize that you are chickens. You made great strides in building a new era. You are the nucleus of the thriving future."

One of them stood to say, "Yes, sir, we know now that we are chickens and we didn't weeks ago. We know now this truth and its meaning. But what will happen next? And what's the new era?"

"All in good time. The second phase ended successfully and I hope that the coming phases will be just the same, fast and successful. Time is short and there is a load of works to do and I fear that death would shoot me with its arrow before finishing what I had started. We must take everyone to there."

"Where sir? How much time was left?"

"Did you say time? Now you know something about time. Your question shows that your intelligence is improving fast and this is what I'm looking for. You'll know everything in good time. The two previous candidates went through these phases slowly. It seems that we are proceeding with an obvious steadiness. Let us get ready for the second phase. Let's go."

8

They were the first days of spring. He woke up at the time of the call to prayer with a liveliness that he didn't feel for so long. The blossoms of flowers were teasing the end of winter that day and the sun came out with its cheerfulness to delight the one his heart wanted. In the meantime, Sahm's heart was rejoicing over the memory of a sincere love. He took Haffar, the eldest of his sons, on a nature walk. They were happy and cheerful for his son graduated from the school of leaders and his degree was conferred upon him by the new teacher specialized in conferring degrees upon farms' leaders according to the news from the Farm Union Complex headed by Abu Rish.

There was a natural harmony between them as they walked; a harmony between a father who was experienced in leadership and aspiring to lead the Union of all hills' farms and his son who was appointed as a delegate of the nearby land. That his son was in power would provide him with support in elections and perhaps he would take his place upon becoming the Governor-General as he was dreaming of.

Or his son might feel tired of waiting; hence, he would disown him once he would sense weakness in him. This was what happened in the world of power at least in the world of chickens. Though he was happy with what this teacher came up with to change the character of this young rooster, he felt threatened by his son, especially that he himself had once overthrown his father. Divine justice might take its course and cast him away.

No, no, I had done that for the good of everyone because my father used to waste wheat to bring white hens from the farms of Man, he thought. His desires used to drain our food that chicks couldn't find a wheat grain or barley for days. I had my excuse. I provided my kids with love, affection and education that would make them take pride in me and support me all my life.

That was his solace in age of distress and suspicion. They walked together with love and harmony overwhelming them in the midst of seriousness and fun, and in the midst of son's expectation and father's aspiration.

From a far, a formation of birds appeared across the horizon. The lines of their formation drawn in the horizon showed that they were migrating. And since they were swimming high across the sky, they were not going to stop to rest in a nearby place. Sahm stared at them which drew the attention of his son who asked, "Why are you staring at that flock of bird, father?"

"Look how beautiful they are; how they fly in a wonderful formation that speaks volumes about unity of the goal and hearts coming together," the father answered.

"O father woe to you. I see that you are fond of this stray group," the son said.

The father, astonished, said," Behave yourself, son."

"Excuse me, father, but you were praising the bitterest of our enemies," the son said.

The father got more astonished. "What enemy son? They are friendly and harmless birds."

"They might be of our breed, but they are not harmless and will never be our friends," the young rooster said.

"They are affable and they have a euphonious voice too," his father said.

"This is the legend that their citizen spies spread. They are a group that deviated from the right path. Their main goal is to get rid of us. We must work diligently to eliminate them," his son said.

"This is undoubtedly a hallucination. Have you eaten any Marijuana grains today that you are babbling on about slander and saying things that have nothing to do with your religious belief?"

"No father, I'm perfectly sane. They are the principles of our lord Nakkar that the first teacher told us," Haffar answered.

"This Nakkar is a historical character. We told his stories to children for the wisdoms and the lessons they contain. And we often read them to children, so that they would fall asleep. It seems that the stories we told you as a child had an immense effect on you," Sahm said.

"Not at all. Our scholars told us that the principles of our lord Nakkar are not legends. Our lord Nakkar personally carved them on the tablets of barley in the depots of the dry grotto at the summit of the last mountain facing the sea of darkness," Haffar answered.

"Didn't I tell you that they are hocus-pocus? Who left and then came back? Be careful son! Don't believe everything you're told …," Sahm said.

"Or what? Did you forget that I'm a distinguished rooster like you! I love you and respect you, but when things get worse I'm going to stand by the side of our lord Nakkar who gave his life for us," Haffar answered.

"Look son, this is a discrimination contrived by members with special ambitions from which they might earn bags and even sacks of wheat and barley. Perhaps they would obtain double yolk eggs to use against us as well. As for birds, I have already met one of them that became dear to me for her decency and civilization and even for her bravery that the world of chickens lacks."

Son: You disappointed me with your saying 'dear'. Children of eagle hate and spite us. They humiliated us and robbed our right. They also were the first to call us children of hen as a disdain rather than as identification. They are the reason why we are so backward that we, of all bird species, feel frustrated and ashamed. I beg you to stay away from them and do not befriend any one of them. They might tempt you that you would bring to us those who deviated from the right path; hence, you will be condemned.

Father: woe to you. You're accusing your father and the leader of the farm of aberrance. You're indeed an undutiful child. I really feel ashamed of your being my son who will rule soon though you have no sense of wisdom or fairness that will help you to survive and thrive. What you're saying has just one futile justification; a leprous teacher whom I barely know.

Son: No father, I have evidence and proof because I met one of them almost a year ago.

Father: What did you find and how did you shape your devilish thoughts?

Son: I found aberrance and atheism; hence I and my friends took revenge on her.

Father: Taking revenge on her?! It's a serious talk...who, when and how???

43

Son: Last year, at the outset of a practical training, we and our teacher were on a training session in the wood studying types of fighting, defending our land and protecting it against enemies.

"Do you mean wolves and jackal?" the father interrupted him.

Son: No, these are familiar enemies and their hostility is linked just to their hunger.

Father: Who, then?

Son: Of course, children of eagle.

Father: You mean eagles. Go ahead, darling.

Son: I rather mean all aerial birds, both small and big ones.

The father, stunned, said, "Go ahead... I can't understand anything anymore; perhaps the rest of the story would clarify the situation."

Son: During our rest near a basil bush, we found a lot of nutritious worms on a tree trunk. We were very hungry after being exhausted by training, so we tried to reach them but our efforts were in vain. We thought of using the small stones that were arranged one on top of the other at one of the basil trees, so we took the pebbles to build for us a hump.

In the meantime, the crest over the head of Sahm was reddening and the purity of his eyes was mingling with the waves of evil that he was hearing as surprise overtook him. He started to pray God secretly that what he was hearing would be a nightmare. And out of wisdom, he didn't say anything but, "go ahead my son."

The son added, "As we were busy with work, the surprise stroke. A spy bird was occupying the place as a center for her operations. But God was with us for divine power inflected an accident upon her which made her unable to accomplish the evil she came for. God protected us from the calamities of their intrigue. And it seems that the spying team left her in a place they thought to be a haven to come back later to her or perhaps they didn't want to move her while she was wounded, so no one would doubt them. But thanks to the blessing of our lord Nakkar we caught her in the act.

Father: Caught her doing what?

Son: She had some of our royal grains and worms we keep for males, especially for wounded warriors to help them recover.

The father said as his anger got fierce, "And then what happened?"

Son: What monumental moments were! The shrewdness of our teacher revealed to us that the bird was but a spy in disguise.

Father: Knowing that the hen belongs to bird species wasn't rocket science.

Son: How kind-hearted you are, father! She is from monitoring agency of children of eagle. Yes, she had samples of our strategic food that includes the rarest and the finest types of worms and grains. And our teacher deduced that since she could reach those stores, her next step must be poisoning the food of leaders to kill them before a few moments of their great attack.

The father: Where did you then take this poor thing?

Sahm didn't hear the answer because of the horrifying shock. The father squatted down thinking of these foolish assumptions of a teacher whom the presidency of the farm sent for a reason that he couldn't figure out. He felt sad for Nagham. He wanted to cry and longed to meet her...he was overtaken by confusion. What would he say or do to know what happened to her? He was only awoken by the voice of his son who said, "We are heroes, aren't we?"

"Of course, you are, son. Still, did you make sure of what the teacher said after interrogating this poor bird," he answered sadly.

"Say the damned bird. We didn't want to take her to the judicial council straight away so that her news would not reach children of eagle; hence, the predatory powers would intervene, thus being spared punishment," his son said.

"How did you punish her, then?" the father said.

Son: We stoned her and opened her wound, so that her punishment would as equal as her crime. She started to moan after she had become unable to cry. We left her in the bush hoping to return to her the next day to quench our grudge before bringing her before justice."

"They are teaching you gloat before proving the guilt!!! And what do you mean by hoping to return. Didn't you return?" his father said angrily.

Son: Hold on, father! I can see that you love female birds. Still, do not be sad for when we returned the following day, we didn't find her.

Father: How couldn't you find her when she couldn't move? Tomorrow I will demand an official investigation. As for you, you will be severely punished at home.

Son: Hold on, father! I was appointed the deputy governor of the nearby farm and I'm no longer the little rooster on whom you could impose your will. I will be inaugurated in a few days and we will become equal. Still, the investigation is carried out with high confidentiality within the halls of the hen-house of rule. They are still studying all evidence to know the inner spy who helped her to smuggle food. I think they are close to arrest the bunch of secret agents and unveil the truth.

Sahm had neither the wisdom nor the power that would help him to keep calm. His crest reddened, his eyesight became blurry and the feather on his head erected .His heart throbbed, or rather wept. He yelled, "Oh you damned! You, your heartless leprous teacher and your stray mates thought that you had crossed the sea of darkness

47

by finding a wounded bird. You changed helping the oppressed with being cruel to them. Why didn't you weave this lie about one of the wolves or dogs? The reason is that you're cowards who want to build glory and history out of lie and hypocrisy at the expense of the weak. I'm the ruler here and I must know what's happening on my farm. I even want to know what is going on in my house.

"I'm smelling threat in your talk!!! Alas!" he added, "I showed you the paths of virtues and morals hoping that you will be the best ruler in the entire world of birds. I want you to be nice to everyone especially the weak and foreigners, but you're threatening me!!"

Son: Here, you say strangers...how did you know that she is one of the strangers?

Father: Alas! Doubt is still in your bosom. You forgot that our conversation started with talking about migrating birds which are strange, didn't you?

The son felt that he was inconsiderate. He was embarrassed too, so he said laughing sincerely, "I'm just teasing you after this tiring argument. You should know that I consider you the wisest and the most honest of all rulers in this Union, father."

He said that adoring his words with a mischievous smile while evil spiders started to link evil threads to each other to weave a lethal cobweb, so that he would be able to rule two farms at once; one he obtained with the help of his father, the other he would inherit from him while alive thus ending up as a national hero once he would bring his father to trial for the accusation of high treason. It was a chance not to be missed. Who would deny his favor if he sacrificed his family for the sake of home land?

Oh! I will be the chief. The devil of power was teasing an ambitious young rooster.

9

Thinking fast and walking slow, the father returned to a private corner where he was used to secluding himself when he went through tough time or when the nagging of his hens increased.

He was born with cluck, lived by clucking, but didn't want to die from nagging. Sorrow and anger fell upon him from all sides. But only the fear of the heart of his undutiful son came mingled with the scent of sadness. He felt scared of his own son. He smelled the scent of treason with a bitter cheerfulness, but he could not say whether it was acquired or inborn. One of them meant that he could win his son no matter what happened, the other things were sadness and crying. Was it too late or rather was it the beginning of a conflict that every king sensed? Obsessions and obsessions were running in the head of someone who was trying to find balance in a world that rode life swings as the fate kept laughing. What was said was an obvious threat to his sovereignty along with his son's direct accusation of treason without any reason which left in his heart a severe bitterness toward an undutiful son. Still, his heart was a hard gate in front of hurricanes. He had first to understand what was going on around him and even how these things were contrived in his kingdom behind his back. In this roaring atmosphere the image of Nagham and her voice echo gave him a surge of strength and energy to figure out their destiny.

Perhaps her destiny was decided and she died or she was suffering somewhere. He didn't know what happened and didn't believe his son's denial of what happened to her.

His eyes wetted. He felt pain, got irritated and plucked some of his feathers...but the throne and the desire to remain in power stirred in him the sleeping ruler. He sharpened his thinking as fast as the flash and thought deeply about the matter. He sometimes smiled at a promising idea and frowned at a miserable one at other times.

After hours of scrutinizing things and balancing thoughts, he was up to something. He returned to the dunghill of rule and sent for the security director, the teacher and his son. He wanted to give everyone a lesson reminding them that he was still the chief. He held a meeting in the hen-house. His eyes moved in two different directions. He observed confidently every crest, stirred in every soul questions and bewildered it. But fear was only inside him and worry overwhelmed his eyes.

He suddenly lifted his head, erected his crest and said, "If anyone doubts my ability to remain in power, let him speak now."

Everyone was stunned and nodded their heads with no. He wasn't waiting for the answer, so he added without paying attention to their answer, "Few hours ago my heir, who was appointed as the deputy of the ninth farm ruler, told me that last year they arrested what is referred to as a secret agent...last year. This happened and I wasn't told or consulted or even informed about this matter. So do you have any explanation for this?" he said looking at the security director.

The security director stood erect and said, "It is a simple matter that we didn't want to bother you with."

Sahm: You say it is simple, while you are involved in torturing a transient bird that disappeared in unnatural circumstances.

Security director: She disappeared without leaving any trace, sir.

Ruler: Why are you continuing the investigation if she disappeared and if the case is foolish? This is what my noble son had told me. He didn't tell me straight away just because he thought that the security director had informed his master about what happened.

He said that trying not to involve his son perhaps his kid wasn't a complicit in the crime and thus he would win him over.

Security director: The matter is out of my hand, sir.

Ruler: Who is in charge here, then?

Security director: You know, sir, that I receive some of my orders from Abu Rish as the supreme commander of the Union of Hill Farms. He ordered me not to inform you about the matter officially.

Ruler: Does Abu Rish doubt my patriotism and my devotion to the world of chickens?

Here the teacher stood to speak, but the ruler did not give him the chance and told him, "Who allowed you to speak? You're here just because you're accused of getting farm children involved in something that will end in tears."

Teacher: Hold on, sir! The case is complicated and what I did was part of my job.

Ruler: You are but a teacher, so don't give yourself a great importance and do not get yourself involved in issues pertaining to ruling.

Teacher: I'm a teacher indeed, but I'm not an ordinary teacher. The Union had invested trough me a great amount of grains in special studies on the farm and nearby farms, so that I would learn what would be beneficial to us in improving productivity, formulating security and planning for the future to provide the needs of farms.

Ruler: You crossed the line by talking like that to a ruler like me belonging to the most glorious farms over ages.

Did all this development take place in bird world, he wondered, and the ruler is the last to know?

Teacher: Excuse me sir. I'm just an employee and what I meant from my talk is that I could help. As for not being informed about what happened, it is the responsibility of supreme committees. It just happened that I was present when the accident took place.

Ruler: How could a terrestrial bird accomplish what you mentioned or understand anything about supreme creatures?

Teacher: Excuse me, sir. I cannot go into these details now. But I assure you that the civilization that son of Adam has been witnessing recently affected us a little bit. For some children of hen became genius thanks to it. We have been left behind since the great disaster, so we must catch up to the civilization that is overwhelming the vast universe. And all that we fear is that it is too late to do so.

Ruler: Hold on! What disaster? We are as good as gold. And where is the vast universe?

Teacher: Excuse me, sir. We are not as good as gold because days are stormy and we have a lot of enemies. It's more complicated than it looks. Tomorrow, I will give an important lecture about this matter for students who graduated days ago to be rulers soon.

Ruler: We're here to deal with a crime, kidnapping and slander not to listen to lectures that may lead us away from the track of finding the truth.

Teacher: Excuse me, sir. Once again I say that I'm just an employee and I came here for a special mission. I think that the lecture will shed too much light on the truth. I will be so delighted with your presence and I think it will later enable us to talk about any aspect of this case.

Suspicion started to get bigger than his small head, but wisdom stirred in his mind. He then said, "It's good to do that for I don't like to be proactive. I hope you wouldn't disappoint me. Let your explanation be sufficient and inclusive enlightening my path with what I had missed."

Everyone then went their way setting hopes on that appointment. Sayah wanted to look deeply into as much information as possible to reach the truth of this secret that he certainly knew it was a slander that was far from the truth. As for the teacher, he shouldered a tough responsibility.

10

On the other side of their world, a group of young white chickens convened in organized rows in front of the eldest among them.

This rooster stood with solemnity and said, "You graduated within a short space of time to be the nucleus of the new world of chickens; a strong and intelligent world in which there is no room for cowardice and subjugation. We are not going to be an easy prey to anyone anymore. We're going to work hard to restore our right to flight. We will live on this planet as equal as all earthly creatures...let's the show begin, so that the chief would see that you're well-prepared for the next phase.

The cheers arose from the very small audience to encourage the new generation. Then the parade started with a group of chickens carrying weapons suiting the nature of their bodies; a scene that was weird and funny for other creatures. And all of a sudden, another group appeared fighting an imaginary enemy and then the parade of using weapons started. It was the first time chickens used a weapon.

The shows of the parade ranged from carrying a picture craved on egg shells to wood sticks carrying strange symbols. Some of them were pictures of the face of an old rooster under which the picture of the great father was craved; others were the pictures of the face of a rooster or a hen. A new world was written on the shells of eggs...a new life and more than that.

The chief looked at the one sitting next to him and said, "It seems that our plan is going well."

"It's your genius that raised our status and took us to another level among creatures," he answered him.

"Yes, this is thanks to the amazing God-given discovery. Still, I'm worried and my worry equals my success."

"O my God! Do you worry after all this?" the one sitting beside him said in an astonished voice.

"I don't know whether it is a permanent change or not, and whether there is a counter reaction or not."

"No matter what happens we are not going to be stupid and cowardly again," the one sitting next to him said.

"I should make sure that all chickens of farms will be able to be like us. I need just time and material together with taking control of natural chickens," the chief answered.

"Wouldn't your plan include original chickens?" the one sitting next to him asked.

"Our conversation stops here. I'm not going to talk about that now. All in good time. But you should know that natural chickens or original ones have been enjoying nature for thousands of years. They have some enemy but that is not serious. However, we were born to be eaten. Every hour millions of hens are hatched in the machines of sons of Adam. They feed us with types of medications to grow quickly and then eat us without any chance to live. What a tragedy!" the chief answered.

"I beg your pardon, sir. That's a painful truth and perhaps God sent you to save everyone, or even to start a new phase," the one sitting next to him said.

"It's OK. Let's enjoy the parade that neither a rooster nor a hen has ever dreamt of. We must become productive partners on this planet," the chief said.

The chief stood and started to greet the paraders and encourage them in their success, promising them with more.

11

The ruler headed toward the dunghill of the rule and stood in that corner that embraced him in crisis, while the teacher took one of these detours in a bypass leading him to the den of the lion without noticing that someone was following him.

Sayah stood atop his dunghill remembering his life events, his passion for a delicate creature, for her affection, her tenderness, her pride, her longing and for the destiny that brought them together.

Is it possible that what he lived wasn't real? Is it possible that love and longing are villainous means to break through the world of chickens? And what of the gunshot? Is it possible that son of Adam is a complicit in the conspiracy of birds? No, it is nonsense.

Moments of stillness prevailed during which he fell silent. But his heart was throbbing, his mind was working with shrewdness and his beak became sharper than at any other time.

Where is the truth? Oh, how couldn't he remember that? Didn't Nagham tell him more than once that he was one of the unprivileged! Didn't she also tell him that he was from an inferior species! No, no, they were jokes. If she meant any word of what she said, she wouldn't give him the impression about the possibility of marrying her. O you poor thing! How is it possible to marry a small bird that is more advanced and more aware of this world than you? Also, she has already told you that she belongs to the breed of Eagle the Great.

His thoughts tossed right and left because it was hard for him to accept the idea of conspiracy against him and against all chickens. He even felt evil coming from the general commander and saw in his son a pervasive wickedness. But the kind side of his heart would tell him, "Perhaps they are victims." However, the other side would tell him, "How can the elite be victims?"

How could his classy and principled beloved be what they were hinting at? No matter who she was, he would not deny what happened between them???Suddenly his pride reigned over the lake of his thoughts.

Here, I'm the king of roosters and chickens and the descendent of a glorious breed. I'm providing my people with nothing but the best. I'm not less than her at all... and she knows that. Everyone around me realizes power and my strength. There is something mysterious I have to figure out what it is. Can this teacher, the informant, come up with answers and proofs to reach the truth? I doubt him too much, but tomorrow is another day that would provide us with answers and explanations.

The white teacher went into the den of the lion with confidence and pride, but the sparks of reverence that the reality of the place radiated caressed his cells. He was seized by fear that was followed by more violent sparks than the memory of his original resident which awakened in him a dormant coward he thought would never wake up. Inside, he found a bunch of roosters waiting for him with a restlessness embodied by a rooster that greeted him and then said, "Why are you late? You worried the white group with your urgent invitation to this strange place...yes, what's the story of this place? No one but you from the world of cowardly chickens would choose such a place."

Teacher: First, I 'm sorry for this urgent invitation, chief, but it is necessary because it touches the core of the case .There is a dramatic turn of events that might blow everything we built. As for the place, I knew that the lion died days ago leaving no heir to occupy it; hence, I took advantage of its reverence, so that our meeting would be held with enough privacy and freedom.

Chief: What do you mean by a dramatic turn of events?

Teacher: As you know, the plan was that I would come here and convince them that I'm a skilled teacher , that my white color was caused by leprosy and that I'm not man-made as they say about us given that we are the products of son of Adam's incubators and farms. And I did that thanks to your instructions. I had moved to the second phase of preparing a new generation of leaders that would be at our command to turn them against the old world and rule the colored chickens forever.

The first group graduated days ago and is about to handle key positions. All that we need is two seasons or three to strike. I told them about the story of the small bird that we found and I took advantage of it to make a national cause out of it.

Chief: I know that, but would you please explain that further to the group because some of them do not know the details and even your incentive for that.

Teacher: You know that colored chickens are very cowardly and I was thinking about taking advantage of this point. And it just happened that I took a group of students for an educational purpose when we found a hen imprisoned under a basil tree surrounded by a pebble fence. May be one of the hunters had an interior motive for imprisoning her. But Haffar, son of Sahm, the president, drew our attention to the presence of royal worms and grains that were ours.

I know this is trivial but I wanted to take advantage of the situation to break the union of this farm for our benefit. Finding the bird in a weird state in the wood in full view of students of military school was a great opportunity for us, especially with what she had in her possession. I used that to fill their hearts with terror by making them believe that aerial birds spite them. I was lucky. I took advantage of the life story of our lord Nakkar and twisted it to suit us. We were about to arrange a solid plan to arrest many rulers using fake evidence as well.

Chief: Great, carry on.

Teacher: Everything was going well until the ruler found out about the accident that took place on his farm. He took it as a challenge to his power, so he got angry and started to dig for origins and branches of the accident. But I smell that he knows something that increases his interest...there is something weird I can smell but I can't tell what it is. The presence of royal food in the possession of a trivial migrating bird requires from us to be cautious because there is undoubtedly someone who brought them to her with a well intention to help. Still, we should bury this concept forever, so that the doer would be a treacherous secret agent.

Chief: I'm fond of your devilish style. What are you going to do, then?

Teacher: I leaked too much information that the story of our lord Nakkar is real not a lie. Many of the residents of the farm and the nearby ones, especially the intellectuals started to consider it a firm reality. Tomorrow, I will give a lecture about this topic. I convinced Sahm to come, but the most important is to use Haffar to dig a grave for his father with his own hands, thus facilitating burying him.

Chief: What made you invite Sahm?

Teacher: His knowing about the matter is the reason. As I have already mentioned, it can destroy everything we had built. We must create a thread between him and this female bird. And from there the thread gets thicker magically thus becoming the hanging rope that we would tie around his neck.

Chief: I don't think that his relation with her is the kind of relation we are looking for. But you have to focus on Haffar to drive a wedge between him and his father which would facilitate our mission. I rely on your devil to do that.

64

Teacher: Yes, but Sahm is intelligent and quick-witted. This is what scares me most because if the truth comes out our role will end and the hopes of white chickens for accomplishing the mission will be dashed. Also, getting rid of racism and degradation with which colored chickens treat us for being the outcome of the manufacture of the civilization of Man is a sublime goal as well.

Chief: We must put personal feelings aside and focus on a mission that is loftier and nobler.

Teacher: But they always call me the leprous teacher.

Here, everyone laughed and one of them said, "Didn't you tell them that you're leprous to accept you?"

Teacher: Yes, and that's what intensifies my grudge against them. I found but spite to put in the heads of the young roosters to win over them. I implanted in them the belief in our lord Nakkar; hence, they began to think that everything I said came from him. They are our secret weapons.

Chief: Great. It is wise that each of us realizes his weapons and uses them for the benefit of our sacred cause. We must put an end to this era of degradation and murder. Do we just exist to be eaten by son of Adam and his dogs and to be humiliated by our own kind? We shouldn't forget that there is a clear goal that we must attain which is taking control of bird world. And for the sake of that, we must be independent to be able to work to acquire the ability to fly thus breaking free of children of Adam, our second enemy after original chickens.

Here, Abu Kamha, one of the members stood and asked, "As the mentor of the group and its future theorist may I ask why you consider the threat that colored chickens pose as our first priority instead of that of Man. The other question is about the possibility of achieving our dream about flying."

Chief: I repeat that Man wants to eat us and take our production of eggs. So if we can stay out of his reach, he would move to another place to satiate his hunger. Our flesh is not the most delicious of birds' but we are less expensive. Man is an easy mission, whereas colored chickens disdain us and treat us as intruders thinking themselves the origin because they come from the creator himself. They want us to be slaves to them and we want freedom. Can't you see a huge difference between freedom and danger? It's so huge.

Abu Kamha: So we must thank Man who made us and cooperate with him.

Chief: Sometimes I doubt your intelligence. Son of Adam made us to eat us not to unite with us.

Abu Kamha: Is that worthy of tiring ourselves out and risking our lives? There aren't too many of colored chickens for that type disappeared. This hill is the only one that contains natural farms that were not built by Man. If we and colored chicken unite together we would survive the cruelty of children of Adam. And if we leave him for a few years, he would perish automatically, or rather we should attract the attention of son of Adam to here.

Here the chief yelled, "Do not even think about it. We need badly the colored chickens. Our life depends on them. I want them alive and spoilt but under our control."

A scary silence fell upon him. The eyes of the chief started to redden and his feathers were fluffed up a little bit. He seemed to be worried more than angry for democracy started to strike a chord with him for he did not expect the discussion to go so far. But his shrewdness saved him, so he looked here and there strictly and said to the crowd, "It doesn't matter whether colored chickens are the first or the last. What matters is that we agree on a plan through which we get the farm ruler onside or get him involved in what would undermine him.

"Let us this tonight carry out a solid plan that would end with our victory. As you know Abu Rish, the chief of the farm, is our secret ally and we will be able to get him involved only when we strike Sahm dead .Yes, time was not important in chicken's world and didn't even exist. But our progress and our reaching this stage of intelligence opened in front of us important horizons. I hope it would be a stage of change for what I hope would be good for children of hen."

They all squatted down and had a heated and an important debate that entailed a dangerous thing that would either lead to success or failure.

Driving a Wedge between…

"Come, son. Let me tell you a secret that I can't keep any longer. I have to pour my heart out to you"- He fell silent for a while- " it's time to clarify the truth," he added after a deep sigh.

Haffar: What truth sir? Did we come to this deserted place to tell me a mysterious truth?

Teacher: Because you are something else and what I'm going to say today is an eternal secret. Still, I promise you that it would be heard by every bird soon. Yes, every flying and walking bird.

Haffar: I thank you for your trust and appreciation, sir. So what happened? You stirred my curiosity.

Teacher: There is an important sentence in the letters and commandments of our lord Nakkar and even one of the most important things mentioned in his commandments which is, 'You will go through a very hard time, my children, that you think there is no escape. You will be killed, slaughtered and tortured with fire to a known day; a day when a victorious rooster that inherited sovereignty from his ancestors will come to save you from every tyrant and oppressor after unveiling the hidden injustice.'

Haffar: Oh my God! A long time has passed since he said that. Is there any hope to find out who's going to save us?

Teacher: We will even be free and fly as he mentioned. We will even take control of this planet.

Haffar: Did he say when the time of liberation would be? Or rather does it have any signs?

Teacher: Yes, he mentioned the signs and everything to come. And I came here just because I knew that this savior appeared and he is ready. We are a bunch of scholars who found out that after examination and scrutiny.

Haffar: Tell me more, sir. I'm longing to listen and to know the savior to be one of his followers.

Teacher: Hold on, sir.

Haffar: What? You are saying sir, sir!!

Teacher: Yes, for you are the so-called savior as sciences mention.

Haffar: Me! It can't be true! It can't be true!

Teacher: I thank you for your humility, sir, but all the evidence points to you.

Haffar: It can't be possible. I know myself better than anyone else.

Teacher: These signs have clues and signals because our lord Nakkar engraved in the grotto behind seas,' An unknown great rooster, that carried glory over ages, will come out from among you to unveil the hidden and kill the bird.'

Haffar: What's hidden and what bird? Really I don't know what you want to say.

Teacher: Aren't you the son of the house that has been ruling chickens for thousands of years? Aren't your inner potentials still hidden inside of you?

Haffar: I undoubtedly come from a glorious ruling house and I don't know whether I have unknown potentials or covered stupidity. Also, my ability might not be in its prime as I'm still young. But this is normal. As for the crux matter of the powerful statement about the hidden and the unknown is in the unseen world.

Teacher: Please sir, I can't tell you more because the situation is more complicated than that.

Haffar: Since you think I'm the so-called savior, tell me what you know.

Teacher: As you wish sir. You were the first to discover the place of the bird that infiltrated into our farm. Hence, you saved us from a vile conspiracy, didn't you? I hope you are the one who will unveil the secret of the great traitor and lead us to safety.

Haffar: Hold on! I don't think that the matter of the bird is important. I discussed this subject with my father and he turned my attention to things from which I realized we misunderstood the course of things. It is not a big deal.

The face of the teacher, who almost drove the wedge between the son and father and split the power, blanched. But the fox that was living between his temples pounced from his face through his tongue and said, "Woe is me, the savior's intuition is never wrong. Our lord Nakkar didn't fail to describe you at all. Besides, unveiling the machination is right. The ability of our master Sahm to convince you that it is a worthless matter is surprising."

Haffar: Woe to you! You're accusing my father and me of things that do not befit us.

Teacher: The first thing that the savior would put in front of his eyes is the nation, the nation of chickens. He must have precognition and wisdom as our scholars said. Secondly, the things I said are facts that should appear for the sake of you, for my sake and for the sake of the nation. When it comes to rule and responsibilities, all are equal. Isn't that what we learned? Also, you have to get rid of tribal fanaticism and family subordination to be the king of the nation to rule and save it or may we, the bunch of scholars, go to hell for failing to interpret for our reverent lord.

He fell silent for a while like someone who was gathering the remnants of thoughts that scattered in the air and put them in a mischievous sentence and then said, "I beg your pardon, sir, for crossing the line, but right is right and I, you and the bunch of scholars are but in the service of the dignified goal."

Haffar: Undoubtedly the principles of our lord Nakkar are fundamental, but my father has the right to my obedience and respect.

Teacher: Yes, my faithful master. But your fate might not be that of your father.

Haffar: Excuse me, dignified teacher, I'm not convinced yet. Still, what is inside of me is scrutinizing what you're saying.

Teacher: It is okay. Let the loyal rooster inside of you speak. Let the good citizen hear the call of duty. Let the savior inside of you come out for we all are longing to meet him. I beg you to ponder on an important question on which our destiny rests. Suppose that the path of your father, the ruler, is different from that of our lord Nakkar, who are you going to support? There is one choice that our lord Nakkar said. Your decision will determine the destiny of the world of chickens or rather all terrestrial feathery birds. I beg you, I beg you, because we are under the mercy of your decision.

The young rooster fell silent with all thoughts rushing to the small course of his thinking. Thoughts of good and those of evil were accumulated; thoughts of avarice and greed thronged, and confused thinking was driven by love for prestige and lust of power.

Is he really the savior? Isn't that what the teacher said on behalf of the council of scholars? And what is my father's role in that? Is it just a suspicion or there is an evidence that would make me confront my father? Perhaps thoughts and doubts about attacking my father sometimes overtook me, but they're just thoughts for I'm not strong and he isn't weak either.

There were endless questions at which the teacher was glancing with insincerity. The teacher saw his eyes bulging east and west, his feather shaking and his crest exploding with redness, so he turned his face away to allow himself a way through which he could take control of the situation more and more. And perhaps his success in driving a wedge between Haffar and his father would dig for him a road through the sea of the chief's pleasure.

Before the evil pie was burned, the teacher wanted to lift it off fire of grudge and intrigue and entrusted to the heart of Haffar, fresh and delicious. He looked at Haffar and asked him, "Who was generous to the nation without expecting anything in return? Was it our lord Nakkar or your father? Who scarified his life for free? Who is going to lead you to glory and loftiness, or rather who is going to provide you with safety on the Day of Judgment? You have to choose, sir, before it's too late. I can't prove more that you are the so-called savior as sciences state. Don't be sad no matter what your choice is, because your father is good and our lord Nakkar is good. Good might be different in form and content, but it is good."

Though these words were characterized by balance, their hidden content made Sahm lose his son's support and pushed the sleeping ruler in him to wake up at the dawn of conspiracy. Yes, there was a way, or rather many ways in front of him to rule and to domineer. But it was shameful to admit even to himself that there was a treacherous race whose roots extended to his being. This teacher found a key for his evil doors.

Haffar stood with extreme pride and a faith imported from treason stores and said, "Reverent teacher, the divine matter that our lord Nakkar predicted started to enlighten my path to guide me to my destiny. I'm not going to disappoint neither you nor your council. I must dedicate my life for the sake of the truth that our lord Nakkar pointed to."

Teacher: Yes, sir, the truth is what we need at the moment; the truth that our existence is at stake. The big conspiracy supported by traitors and murderers, the essence of which is unknown for us. We must know the big truth about our inability to fly, or rather how we're going to fly. I will always be your assistant and faithful counselor.

Haffar: Certainly, you will always stand by my side until we reach our goal. But I must seclude myself to know where I'm going to start my search of the truth.

Teacher: God bless you, sir. Go to your retreat and think again about the accident's details; the accident of the bird with its previous and coming details. Look at the ends of the threads perhaps you would guide us to the traitors who leaked the royal food.

Haffar: See you soon.

Teacher: See you soon, sir.

13

A bunch of male chickens or roosters as they were referred to, were convening. All of them would occupy key positions from a small farm governor to a prominent security officer. But they would definitely end up in an important world. First, they were scarce in the world of chickens. Second, they were the cream of the males of the second generation. Third they would marry the biggest number of hens. There were in front of them a high-ranking official who was our friend Sahm, the ruler, known exclusively as Sayah. No one but I and you know this name, dear reader, and of course Nagham.

Did you forget her? If you did, Sayah would scream at, "I came here and swallowed my pride just for her!! If she died or disappeared, I have to bring back her dignity especially in front of my son. I'm not going to accept her death until that leprous teacher dies after drawing the truth from any spot of his body."

While Sayah was absorbed in his thoughts and memories, the white teacher climbed to a high pile of dry dung of chickens that made him visible to the attendees on the dunghill of meeting. He gazed at everyone until his eyes met those of Sahm. His face brightened up and he said, "I would like to thank his Excellency, the ruler, who is honored to have us here as an encouragement for knowledge. This lecture is so special first because of the presence of my lord, the ruler. Second, it will inform future rulers about the truth about our fate linked with knowledge, and enlighten them about who we are, what we are made for and why progress disease hasn't affected the world of chickens yet.

"Our hens lay eggs and hatch, while we crow and mate. The result is that they all feed on us that we are about to disappear. We are the only ones left from natural chickens on this hill along with some chickens scattered here and there. The only hope for survival that children of hen have is you. Yes, there are white chickens and most of them do not know that they are chickens. They were born and then Man fed them food and medications that would swell them and increase their flesh and weight to kill them after three weeks. They don't live long enough to have a fully-developed mind. Here you are doing your best thanks to this prudent leader and the wise leadership of the group of the Union of Farms to see your chicks, roosters and hens after months and even to see your grandchildren having fun and playing. Afterward, a wolf or a fox, not to mention son of Adam would take their life to satiate his appetite by killing and eating. Do you want to continue in this miserable condition?"

Students screamed, "No, no. What's the solution, then?"

The teacher looked at them with challenge and added, "First you have to ask 'why not?', and then 'What is the solution?'"

He fell silent as his eyes were roaming across the room observing the reaction of everyone, then he continued by saying, "Thousands years ago, there were no birds at all; neither aerial nor terrestrial. We used to be known as the feathery because our body was covered with feathers instead of wool or hair to protect us and keep us warm. We used to have hands with little fingers covered with feathers we call now wings."

His eyes started to roam over the audience to see the impact of the shock and he secretly noticed that Sahm wasn't interested as he knew that what had been said so far was just the introduction of the imaginary life story of our lord Nakkar. Sahm didn't know how the lecture would be like with the beginning of a meeting the clouds of which did not predict rain. But the teacher went on to say, "You will say that the elevation theory does not apply to all creatures. Why did all feathery birds develop into a more sublime being except us and a few feathery birds like ostriches and turkeys? The theory is not wrong. No, then no. It is a conspiracy.

What we're going through now is the outcome of the Grain Valley Pact between children of eagle and the hoary witch.

Here Sahm stood and said in a loud voice, "We didn't come here to mix children stories with politics and the nation's destination. Forget about these superstitions."

Teacher: No, sir. It is not. This is what they want us to believe, those impudent secret agents who kill us every day. There is no doubt that there are intelligent scientists who devoted their life to attaining the truth in our nation. Recently, tablets engraved on barley plates with Nakkarian language have been discovered in one of the dry grottos at the southern entrance of the desert. Children of eagle conspired against us and sold us forever to the enemy. Yes, the story is written in details.

One of the youths stood and said, "What's that story? Do we have the right to know it?"

The orator added, "I invited you to this lecture just to unveil the truth upon instructions from the President of the Union of Farms Abu Orf. I'm disclosing the truth for the first time outside the strategic center upon the instructions from my lord Abu Orf as I have already mentioned, so that our future would be better when a class that is aware of the truth comes to power thus leading us to safety with the guidance of my lord, the ruler of this farm."

Then he looked at Sahm while bending his head. Everyone in the room greeted him, so he looked at them gratefully as his crest erected with its usual pride and his eyes roamed in every direction wondering about the truth about what's happening.

The teacher looked intently with a scrutinizing eye to find Haffar and give him affectionate gazes carried by a messenger of guile from the eye of shrewdness, but he didn't find him.

He was confused a bit and worried a lot for a few moments. Still, he would not give the attendees a chance to notice his absent-mindedness, so he drew confusion gazes into himself, swallowed them reluctantly and then continued to speak, "Let me read for you a copy of the original text of the pact that resulted in our situation. Our lord Nakkar got its sample copy through the wife of Eagle the First, as her origin traced back to children of hen.

"She felt the oppression that was inflected upon her own kind, so she sent this copy to our lord Nakkar the First warning him about the conspiracy woven against him and against children of hen.

The text states, 'This is a perpetual agreement between the hoary witch on behalf of mankind and Nisr Abu Al-Makhaleb on behalf of every feathery bird. The two sides stroke this agreement in the seventh universal year and it is an agreement that cannot be broken. It was witnessed by spirits and ghosts, so if one of the two sides terminates it, his life would be destroyed, his species would perish and his progeny would eternally live in hell.

1. Feathery birds should give up on acknowledging the following species and eternally abandon them: chickens, turkeys, geese, ducks, and ostriches. Other species could be added in a week in a list agreed on with Nisr Abu Al-Makhaleb, the chief of feathery birds.

2. Man can benefit from the eggs and meat of these abandoned species through the means he thinks is suitable either through eating or pleasure or torture.

3. What is left of feathery birds can have what would enable them to fly eternally in the sky and move wherever they want either by land or by air.

4. Most small feathery birds have special vocal cords that would compensate for their loss.

5. Son of Adam has the right to hunt what would become a bird after this agreement becomes operative. Birds have the right to destroy or use the properties of son of Adam or attack him. There should be no opposition to this or that for the vital interests of both sides.

6. Feathery birds whose names are not mentioned in the first clause would convene in a month in the great plain so that the witch would read the necessary

81

talismans and give them satanic barley enabling them to fly.

It was agreed and signed on what have been mentioned with the consent of the committee of feathery birds and delegates of children of Adam headed by Nisr Abu Al-Makhaleb and the hoary witch.

P.S. Nisr Abu Al-Makhaleb expressed his opposition to the word torture mentioned in the second clause.

So, children of Adam decided after many deliberations that torture would be merciful. And this decision warmed the heart of the group of feathery birds after they made sure that their own kind would be fine.'"

The teacher fell silent to see the surprise in everyone's eyes, and then said, "That's what happened. There is no comment but you are the future. You know the truth now, so dedicate your life to raising the banner of the nation and to restoring its rights. And that could only be achieved through working hard and standing by the side of the savior when he shows up to show us the truth."

Everyone was surprised at hearing the word savior. They, astonished, shouted disapprovingly at once, "The savior"

"Yes, yes. It is the glad tiding of our lord Nakkar as it will be the ship rescuing us from backwardness and machinations toward sublime freedom," the teacher said.

Here Sahm stood upset and said, "This is too much. What you're saying is too much. I didn't hear that there is a savior, or rather I didn't know that we need a savior. Aren't we the same as we came into this world that is before our lord Nakkar himself was born? What's new now? This is a false article."

"I beg your pardon, sir. These are the words of our lord Nakkar. They are in the dry grotto and you can see them whenever you want," the teacher said calmly.

Sahm: That grotto is very far. It takes months to go there. Let us be realistic for I put up with the first story reluctantly, but I couldn't endure this one.

Teacher: Hold on sir! Knowledge is a vast sea and our scientists work hard day and night for your sake, for my sake and for the sake of all children of hen. Also, clear signs that were predicted by our lord Nakkar start to appear. We are waiting for him to show up...perhaps you would be the savior.

Sahm: No comment. I have to make sure of this nonsense.

Teacher: Thank you all. May peace and God's mercy be upon you.

Chickens fluttered their wings. They greeted him and praised both Sahm, the ruler, and Abu

Orf, the chief. Sahm stood thanking their greeting, then turned to the teacher with a fake smile on his face that the teacher answered with a mischievous one.

Sahm was distracted by what he had heard. It was true that he heard the lecture, but what he heard couldn't be processed by his mind. He didn't accept it because it seemed odd. It was the word savior that annoyed him most as it was misplaced. But the faith in his heart and the reverence of our lord Nakkar left thin threads; perhaps they would link the miracles of the pious with the words of the mischievous to be in favor of public interest. He always left a room for discussion, because a wise ruler would predict what was unexpected.

Is it possible that a chief like me, who hears news about far places and strange stories, doesn't know such a highly-important, dangerous matter? It is weird.

However, the leprous teacher boasted secretly about his shrewdness and intelligence.

The scheme was working. If the ruler believes my talk or some of it, he will be in the game. He didn't have any doubt that the high council and Abu Orf would accept him as a partner in their undertaking. But if he has any doubt, he would have to go to the dry grotto that didn't exist to make sure of that. There, everyone would be happy to get rid of him.

The teacher approached the ruler and said, "I'm at your command to meet whenever you want to continue yesterday's discussion over the unresolved case."

This villain is but a hidden hand of Abu Orf. I have to gain time and collect information, Sahm thought. Then he looked at his lecturer and said, "You did very well tonight and made my suspicious go away. I have to think about the matter of this savior. I have to think deeply about the savior and what could be saved. Since I'm tired tonight, I hope I will have the chance to meet you tomorrow or the day after tomorrow. I will send for you. Goodbye."

The teacher said, astonished, "Goodbye."

14

The teacher stayed with his students discussing the lecture. And once they dispersed, he called the dearest of them all to kill time that he didn't know where to spend. He wanted to be late to make sure that the place would be empty thus guaranteeing his leaving without being followed. As for Sahm, he went out. A headache was teasing his temples surrounding this small head. How could a simple accident full of love and tenderness change into a groundless national issue? He took pride in his throne. He had what it took to rule this farm and other ones including loyal powerful guards and intelligence. In spite of that, a strange teacher came to pose a real threat to him!!How could that happen?

How couldn't I figure out that he came to turn our chicks into roosters carrying thoughts and opinions that had nothing to do with our surrounding? He made them the way he wanted or the way his masters who brought him ordered him.

Oh, Abu Rish, how wicked he is! But Abu Rish is a noble and kind rooster that cares only about his desires. Yes, perhaps he didn't understand or realize where this teacher comes from and even why he comes in the first place. Oh, they entered through a door that Abu Rish didn't perceive, and even I didn't perceive, an unexpected door; our secrets from the mouth of our kids. He knows too much and his danger is undoubtedly huge. Oh! It's a complicated case that triggers the mind and would cost too much. It affects ruling, heart, home and every member of children of hen. It touches our sacredness.

He asked Katkout to come quickly. This Katkout was a small rooster as old as his son, but his physical development wasn't complete, so he looked like a chick. Still, he was sharp-witted and insightful. He could be relied on to do tough missions as well.

"I want you to follow that white teacher wherever he may go, and to heed, understand and report every single word you hear."

Katkout: Yes, sir. I followed him yesterday for I felt suspicious when I saw him taking a strange path.

Ruler: What did you find?

Katkout: I saw him approaching the den of the lion, so I ran away. He must be retarded. Who will go with his own free will to the den of the lion? I was surprised to find him alive today!

Ruler: This is what I was looking for. Follow him wherever he goes even if goes to the lion's heart...

Katkout: I can't do that sir. I don't want to die.

Ruler: Do not be afraid, dear. If that damned teacher didn't die, then you won't. Still, you should know that the lion died weeks ago and it seems that he knows that. He is hiding something there. He is wicked.

Katkout: Your wish is my command, sir.

In the small hours when children of the other side were playing with lamps that were decorating the galaxy dress lighting up the path of lovers, teasing their longing with colors, which thrived and then dimmed to impart a touch of tenderness to the restless, Sahm was in one of the corners of his retreat absorbed in looking at the fast events and the contradictory questions that swayed before his eyes.

Facts were mocking him. How couldn't he see them while they were there all the time? How didn't he care about his being and existence? Where did he come from and where was he going? Was it true that he was a descendant of those whose right was violated? If history was different, would he play with butterflies along the breeze wings in these moments? Would he meet Nagham in space? Would they live together on one of the clouds or would they fly over flower forests joyously?

Dreams overtook him for a while. He was elated for moments that took him to another world of freedom and start.

But even if what he heard wasn't true, why wouldn't he ever think about the sky? Why didn't his ambition take him from this tedious life to challenge and to the highest status of success? Hold on! How would I fly when I was doomed to be a rooster like every rooster and hen since the beginning of time? But Man didn't fly before and didn't have any wings. He created the means with a strong will, thus fulfilling a dream. Weren't we with Man when he was in the woods being chased by wolves and dogs as they were chasing us? There is something we, children of hen, lack.

He retreated into himself and then went back to reality.

What if the teacher's talk is right? What if he proves his truthfulness? Is it possible that Nagham can be a secret agent? Is it possible that there is among birds one of those who think about hatred, hostility and killing like son of Adam? Some birds are predatory. They hunt us sometimes, but they have never posed a threat to us. Are they like that by nature or what? Is it logical that Nagham put her life in danger, so that things would look natural? Isn't it possible that the music of her voice is but screams of ecstasy for winning a prey? It is one hell of a prey. It is an entire world. And if the things I missed are true, how would I justify my helping her? Oh my God, how lowlife I am to let

89

evil thought affect our true love. No, no the reality is different from what they are saying. We're two lovers from two different worlds, and that unites us not parts us. No one can tarnish my love. The mere thinking of their words is but a desecration of the sacredness of our love. Oh my God! How lost I am! What shall I do? What shall I do?

He fell apart exhausted and lost under the lanterns of the sky unaware of the truth in two strange worlds with bitter realities. And his feeling of bitterness for feeling guilty was powerful because he had never thought of becoming a better being.

"Isn't there any solution? Isn't there any ally that would open my hopes and increase my understanding?" he said with longing for knowledge and hope for reaching the truth.

All of a sudden, he smiled and screamed, "I found it, I found a glimmer of hope...an ember of light. Yes, the only one capable of standing by my side in such a situation is Zaghloul, the hermit, the sheikh of scholars and even the most famous of all birds whose opinion is forced upon everyone. Let's go to him, Sayah. He's on the nearby hill."

The hermitage was at the highest point of the nearby hill, on which lay a giant tree as old as the soil in which it grew. There was in it a tree house built by faith legends and rebuilt by sincerity of worship whenever solidarity was eaten away by creatures. Zaghloul had been in this hermitage since the beginning of time carrying his prayers to God from this humble lodgment. There was always Zaghloul that was always a hoopoe carrying an inner intuition and an obvious delicacy.

Zaghloul would wait for anyone to ask him a question. If he didn't have an answer in his heart, he would pray for him, do anything, so that he would not return empty-handed. He would give medication to this and a book to that. If his senses failed to find a solution or a cure, he would then pray for his visitor at the very least. He was a God-fearing sage. His visitors ranged from a hen that could not lay eggs to an eagle that didn't touch stars apart from a coward lion and a tuneless bird. Sahm stood on the trunk of the old willow, with his feet on the ground and his head in the sky looking at the window of the tree house in which lived the hermit to call out to him once there was a hint that he woke up. He arrived before dawn break; perhaps the dawn of truth would appear.

It didn't take long until a bird with a crown of arranged and sparkling feathers on his head appeared. His morning face lighted the dark willow leaves up. Sahm wanted to scream to call out to him, but the reverence of the place imposed on him silence. After waiting for gentle moments which he felt like a lifetime spent in a temple, he heard someone calling out to him, "Oh honored brother, do you need any help?"

"Yes, my lord. I need your wisdom perhaps you would bring back whom I lost or whom I miss." Sahm answered him with the eagerness of a yearner.

"Welcome. I hope I won't disappoint you," the hermit said that. "I will come down and listen to you with a sympathetic ear.

Sahm : It's generous and noble of you to do that.

The hermit swaggered fluttering, then perched on a rock as high as Sahm. He looked at Sahm with scrutinizing eyes, raised his head a bit and then said "Welcome to our expanse of land. I hope I will be rewarded because of you."

Sahm: Thanks for your landing on the rock. As it is known I cannot fly and what you did shows how humble the highly- knowledgeable hermit is. I inform you that the power is about to be lost and taking hold of things becomes hard, and thus I'm no longer able to keep this or hold that.

Hermit: It seems that you are a descendant of a collapsing prosperous house. How could I figure out how I can help you if richness has never been one of my goals?

It is clear that I'm in the presence of someone who mocks me in these moments but...

"Yes sir. I'm from the nearby hill and my name is Sahm. I didn't come here for a material or a personal matter for the greatest of things are different from this and that even if it didn't seem so."

Hermit: It seems that you have your own share of wisdom...go on.

Sahm: Thanks, sir. I came here to know if your bird species always takes control of the sky; hence, you can fly wherever and whenever you want. I mean is your ability to fly innate or acquired?

Hermit: Ha! That explains your saying I can't fly instead of saying I don't fly.

Sahm: I've never thought about the sentence. Still, this means I'm in safe hands.

Hermit: May be you didn't do that, but there is in your subconscious mind an inner intuition bringing you back to your centre of interests. Still, no master like you has ever come before dawn break to ask a question that wouldn't change anything. What's the story, dear, so that my answer would have a relevance to what kept you awake?

Sahm: I thought so, until yesterday when I heard the story of our lord Nakkar and his relation with Nisr Abu Al-Makhaleb in a text that is new to me. I don't mean the frequent story, but rather history. I then was afraid that my ability would be double; inability to fly and to understand.

Hermit: History is not scary. As for the story that the world of chickens was circulating is a mixture of delusion and imagination. Some of it was built for wisdom; some of it was built for filling emptiness.

Sahm: Is there a part which is true? For you're giving us names I don't know at all like children of hen. And there is even a bird that is dear to my heart described me as underprivileged, or rather one of the underprivileged. I didn't know the meaning then, but it seems that attributes increase and history mingles with legends.

Hermit: Yes, legends and history have always been intertwined. History is written by the one that wins the war, while legends were written by the crowd to express their hopes. But there are always documents, inscriptions and traces that the claims of the victor and poems of dreamers cannot change.

Sahm: When truth mingles with fantasy, delusion gets bigger and we live it with happiness. Our dreams get as big as our understanding; hence, we end up in an imaginary world and fail to differentiate between reality and fantasy, between the words of the victor and the dreams of the crowd. And when the truth sun rises, the claims of this would fall apart and the legends of that would wither, and thus commoners announce the truth because it takes them out of their delusion. Therefore, they all become victims of the truth which they were expecting to warm their heart. Isn't fair that the truth becomes subject to hatred and we even set it up to be a defendant to die by hanging with the noose of our lies.

Hermit: It seems that you're not one of the masters. You are the master.

Sahm: Thanks, sir, for this compliment and recognition.

Zaghloul: Never mind that now! I think you came here for a strong reason that concerns an entire nation as I understood. Tell me about your obsessions. I can help you.

Sahm: Yes, reverent hermit. There is someone who wants to hurt us, we, the farm chickens. We don't know who he is or what his nature is; an enemy that uses the weapon of racism, grudge and revenge as if he took revenge for an unknown thing. My intuition tells me that it's a disaster that is going to affect the world of chickens first, and then will spread like fire burning hay to affect even eagles in their skies. Revealing the truth requires a tremendous work.

Zaghloul: Yes, events that are not ordinary require unordinary decisions from unordinary creatures. Let's go back to Abu Nisr Abu Al-Makhaleb. The legend, which children of hen were narrating, especially the life story of our lord Nakkar was immensely twisted. Though there are a lot of icons and traditions in it, it is a far cry from reality.

Sahm: Do you mean that they only meet at the beginning and the end?

Zaghloul: Sort of, but the historical truth mentioned in our old records and your guarded ones by the biggest of scholars are different from the life story circulated by beaks.

He fell silent a bit as if he wanted Sahm to record in his cells every word that would be the truth he harvested in his lifetime. He closed his eyes for seconds that were enough to regain the past pictures that were absent from his body. His eyes glittered to say that they were going to start...and he started, "In old time, as old as the existence of souls on this planet, there were creatures moving on the ground, others dived in water. As for the sky, the Phoenician and Greek children of Adam said it was a stage that was restricted to deity. However, we, feathery birds, used to move on the ground and knew but clouds and rains of the sky.

"We were the common point between Man and animal. Everyone was fighting to attack us and simply put us on his table. We sadly were the cheapest of food and the easiest to be hunted. Maybe you realize better than me the fear waves that flow in the cells of the one that knows he will be killed or hung or burned or trampled any moment and will be up for grabs by dirty mouths. Fear was our air and terror was our fate as it was the fate of every feathery bird. We have remained so for thousands of years until that distinctive day came."

Sahm: What do you mean by distinctive?

Zaghloul: A day that distinguished between our presence as slaves on the surface of nature and our moving to be the masters of the sky. That day, our lord Nisr Abu Al-Makhaleb, a big chicken, was walking happily in one of African plains when the roar of an angry and hungry lion terrified him.

Abu Al-Makhaleb saw him running and the ground was folding for him as if it was jelly. He saw his mouth open, and between the folds of it, sharp teeth were sparkling being carried by a hungry face looking for a prey. He was carried over the wind by hard pointed claws in fast feet. Abu Al-Makhaleb realized that he was the intended prey. Abu Al-Makhaleb wasn't a coward. Though fear overtook him, there was inside of him a creature that wanted to have a decent life for himself and for his family.

He was the chief of his people and he was not supposed to be eaten. He realized the limits of his power among feathery birds, and that's why he felt that running might stop that beast. He started to run and run spreading his wings high. He wanted to make the lion believe that he was his equal; hence, he would go away. But the lion kept running and distances started to shrink. So, Abu Al-Makhaleb started to move his wings fast to make himself look stronger in a battlefield in which he was weak.

All of a sudden he saw himself rising from the ground and going far in the space to a distance that the lion didn't dream of reaching. He was terrified by what he saw and thought that the deity took his life. He started to see things from another perspective; a new world emerged and horizons opened. He even went to another side. Also, his imbalance and instability made him fall in the perceptual disorder. Honestly, he ended up in a world he wasn't familiar with. He couldn't see the lion, so he was overtaken by joy. He stopped moving and started to swing in space. He turned around himself in a fast twirl and saw the ground rushing toward him until he fell unconscious.

Sahm: What a strange story! I hope I find in its end a comfort for my sleeplessness.

Zaghloul: This is only the beginning and I promise you that your answer will be sufficient.

When he woke up, he found himself in a strange place far from the earth and creatures he was familiar with. He sat thinking deeply about what happened. Was it magic or was it the deity who dragged him to her then threw him away from her and from his family for a reason he didn't know. He sat for days thinking about what happened and even how it happened. Eventually, he was guided to take it as simply as it is. In other words he flew; therefore, he was saved from the lion and he had to know how that happened. He realized that this was the sharpest weapon in his hand to face whoever wanted to hurt him. He started to imagine the lion attacking him, so he ran and ran resuming a role that he performed as best as it could be done.

Success and failure mingled in his attempt until he found himself flying short distances, then longer and longer until he started to fly distances taking him from one hill to another. He felt happiness and power and started to take control of air undisputedly; peerless and all alone. But loneliness in space bothered him, and his longing for his family caught him. He couldn't return...he wasn't the same anymore, he was a new creature.

After long months, he landed at the place of our grandfather Zaghloul the first who couldn't fly but he was definitely a great sage. Abu Al-Makhaleb told him about what he was going through, about his sleeplessness, and about his new weapon and what he could do with it. He displayed his new gift in front of him and told him about the benefits of taking control of the earth.

Zaghloul the Great suggested that this blessing was a chance not to be missed by feathery birds and that he had to teach it to every bird. Our lord Abu Al-Makhaleb hesitated a bit then suggested teaching eagles first. Zaghloul told him that by doing so, he would sin and be cursed by deity. He was stunned by such talk from someone toward whom he felt love and respect. So, Zaghloul said that soul was prone to evil, so if he saw his children and grandchildren playing in space and making their houses at the top of trees, he would feel arrogant and be overtaken by might; hence he would not teach anyone. He told him then that the sky was vast and teaching one member is like teaching many. He listened to his opinion and chose some birds for trial.

My grandfather was one of them and after a while, a team invited delegates from all kinds of feathery birds. He paraded in front of them with his few students and offered to teach them what he knew till space would become theirs until the day of resurrection.

Sahm: I understand. All birds but chickens learned to fly either because they didn't accept the invitation or because they weren't invited in the first place.

Zaghloul: Hold on! It is neither this nor that. I thought you're wise in the beginning, didn't I? I hope you remain so till you leave.

Sahm: I think that wisdom sometimes abandons the heart of its bearer.

Zaghloul: Here it comes back quickly. It's okay. After the explanation of Nisr Abu Al-Makhaleb and the parade, they were stunned and belied what they saw with their own eyes. But they soon gave in to the truth that promised them a new world; a world of freedom and power they had never thought of. Surprise took them from reality to weird dreams, but the wisdom of Nisr Abu Al-Makhaleb was overpowering, so he said to them, 'Let everyone of you discuss the matter with his people for a few days after which we will meet here.'

Each of them went back to his small world, talked, convinced and tried hard. You even can say that some of them fought to convince their people. It wasn't easy to convince anyone to accept the impossible. Flying was impossible and even thinking about it might be forbidden... the sky was only for the deity. But they came on time and practiced with patience and effort till all of them flew and in few months, the sky was crowded with them.

Sahm: What does this have to do with me?

Zaghloul: Our lord Nakkar was a knowledgeable sage. He wasn't only the master of chickens, but also the master of chickens, ducks, geese and others. He tried to convince them, but it was in vain. They were scared and terrified from falling or angering the deity. After long consultations, the group of chickens decided to send a delegation from all teams to try what is forbidden.

Sahm: Yes, they went. Why didn't they fly, then?

Zaghloul: Hold on! Be patient, dear. On their way, the delegates started to convene in secret discussions far from our lord Nakkar who was keeping an eye on them. They thought of accusing him of agreeing with Nisr Abu Al-Makhaleb to sacrifice them to the Phoenix or to offer them as scapegoats to the deity. Finally, they agreed to satisfy him until they would get rid of him forever.

Our lord Nakkar represented a nightmare for them. Once they arrived at the field of training and met Nisr Abu Al-Makhaleb, they expressed their approval. But at the emergence of the first threads of dawn, the bunch sneaked to the dunghill of our lord Nakkar to kill him. They tried to stab him with their beaks as hard as possible; they poked all his body and plucked his feathers. He couldn't fight

101

this large number of chickens, so he tried to run away to the wood half-naked with no feather covering him. Everyone in the plain saw him from afar running toward the wood to hide among its shrubs forever. His people were running after him saying, 'We're not leaving you, we're not leaving you.' So, everyone in the pain thought that he ran out of fear and that his species was comforting him.

Sahm: So, his own species and his allies killed him. Oh my God, what a disaster!

Zaghloul: Yes, he never came back home, but left for my grandfather Zaghloul the Great a trace in the form of an inscription on a tree trunk depicting the accident.

Sahm: How come that you blame us and accuse us of cowardice and fear?

Zaghloul: When the killers left the place of the accident with joy overwhelming them for getting rid of a master whom each of them was aspiring to replace, they were heedless of what might result from their action. But once the features of their homes started to appear in the horizon, they were faced by the serenity of confessing their crime, so they stood silent in their places.

They wanted to agree on one lie because our lord Nakkar was wise, composed and strong. They remained as such until one of the Satan of lying appeared on the tongue of one of them and said, 'We say he was terrified by the sight when he knew that he was about to jump from the top, and since he was old, he couldn't stand the shock; hence, worry made him feel scared, so he ran to the wood where we found him dead from terror. Yes, ask everyone in the plain who saw him when running away to the wood as we were running behind him saying we're not going to leave you alone forever because we are your family and your own kind.' After hearing it, everyone yelled, 'Yes, yes that's what happened. Then they let out a victorious laugh.

Sahm: Didn't anyone ask them why they didn't practice flying?

Zaghloul: Yes, and their answer was ,'We felt ashamed to meet anyone after the humiliation and disgrace that were inflected upon us by our lord Nakkar, so we decided to go away and not to see anyone to save face.'

Sahm: And what does this have to do with me? Where is my answer for accusing us with cowardice?

Zaghloul: Cowardice is not innate in you. It's acquired. It enters into you through stories and rumors spread by terrestrial and aerial birds. The story, which some members invented for hidden reason wrapped with story of fear and cowardice, became a part of your story, so cowardice became the good citizen and even fear became one of patriotism's qualities. Look at any hen of your own kind how she is facing the entire universe to defend her chicks.

If fear is innate in them, they wouldn't be able to do so. Those who claimed cowardice and fear and those who stuck faint-heartedness to our lord Nakkar did so mainly to serve personal interests. There is a thin thread separating truth from others.

Look inside of you. If you find a bird that wants to launch, help him to break free and let him be the nucleus, so that your own kind would walk in our footsteps, and thus you would save the truth from being a legend whose goal is to put you in the prison of lack of will with your fearful jailors. Go, son, carry the truth in your heart, water it with your honesty and love it more, perhaps you will reach your goal. Goodbye.

Sahm: Goodbye. Perhaps we would meet in your tree house...yes in your tree house.

15

A few days passed during which the teacher was the most worried and bewildered of all chickens. He was looking for Haffar everywhere, but it was in vain. There was a load of work to do. Haffar became an important pawn of these of chess scattered in his game. The rules of the game required from him to play now for if he delayed, he would lose everything. He had to move Haffar to tie the hands and the feet of the king before the king would say to him, "Checkmate!"

Sahm too couldn't find his dear son. He wanted to kiss him and spread his wings over him which broke his heart. Also, he wanted to talk to him about the course of events, and the most important reason was the hopes he was setting on his son to help him solve the enigma of a love story that he and Nagham started and did not know how it would change into a conflict between members of the same house.

The chief of his guards and Katkout could not find Haffar anywhere. No one saw him for a while even the important lecture in the presence of his father, the farm ruler, did not attest to his presence. Sahm was pinning high hopes on his son to be his support, while the teacher was building an edifice with an astounding future that the chief blessed besides praising his thoughts and enlightening him with some orders and instructions perhaps they would lead them to victory, or rather to dominance. It was a matter of existence.

One evening the moon died and the stars hid their bright out of grief over it for a while. In a few moments the sky started its delivery of a new moon, and thus the stars rejoiced and released their brightness here and there celebrating the new moon. In the meantime, on the earth, on a nearby hill, the sounds of fast steps followed near the dunghill of Sahm. He was overtaken by suspicion. He looked here and there and asked, "Who is there?"

"Do not panic. I'm Haffar, your son."

Father: Where were you, my son? I was so worried about you.

Son: I'm fine and even better than any time.

Father: Where were you? What is the result of this long absence?

Son: Only good things happened. I came to you to talk perhaps good things would increase or...

Father: Or what, my son?

Son: Nothing, father...I was occupied with the matter of the spy bird.

Sayah was overtaken by surprise that he couldn't find anything to say but, "It is a trivial matter, while you are the hope for happiness and inner peace."

Haffar: It is a good start for me to be like that, father.

Sahm: Do you have any doubts about that?

Haffar: Honestly, yes...

Sahm: Yes!!!

Haffar : I do not doubt your love and hope, but rather doubt your answering my doubts frankly, so that I could make you happy.

Sahm: Answer what?

Haffar: I pondered on the incident of the bird deeply and found but one truth; the bird is a wounded spy hidden on our farm with our gains and royal worms in her possession. How did she make it to here and who helped her?

Sahm: Of course we will find an explanation if we think deeply and looked for reasons.

Haffar: The only explanation is that she was wounded and then hid in our land. Someone helped her, which brings up the question: Is he a double agent for her own kind or a fool from his own kind.

Sahm: Let us discuss this matter together again.

Haffar: I tried to talk to you and I always seize your defending her and her own kind as if you were one of them. I even have never seen one rooster that knows a bird except you. Isn't it suspicious?

Sahm: What do you mean, my son? It seems that you mean me by one of the qualities of treason and stupidity.

Haffar: No, I wasn't hinting at you by this quality or that. I mean that you always say that you have a friend among them; that they are your friends and that we are all birds as if you didn't distinguish between a flying bird and a flightless one.

Sahm: Of course, I don't because that's the truth. Some of us fly, some don't. And the other truth is that they haven't done anything wrong to us over years. We even rarely notice their landing at our land.

Haffar: Excuse me, father, your defense shows that you are hiding something suspicious. You even might be the one who helped her.

Sahm: This is a clear accusation.

Haffar: I didn't mean it that way. I'm just saying that nothing is in your favor. And I'm afraid for you because the truth will come out once studying the prints of beaks is finished.

Sahm: Let us wait.

Haffar: Wait for what? If they don't find a print that matches those of the crowd including chickens and roosters, Abu Rish will give an order to examine the prints of the rulers.

Sahm: I see that you and the teacher work hard to hurt me just for a suspicion I don't know where it comes from.

Haffar: I doing my best to save this nation.

Sahm: Saving it from what exactly!?

Haffar: I'm not certain, but I have an intuition that there is a threat surrounding it that pushes me to work hard to save it. I have to find out what's happening and work to stop the schemes of damned birds. I have to save children of hen.

Sahm: Oh my God! My son wants to save chickens and the teacher wants a savior.

Haffar: Shall I tell you the truth?

Sahm: What truth? All that he said in the lecture that you didn't attend was that there is a savior who will rush to our help. It's a ridiculous idea. How would a character that we have never heard about emerge? It's a big lie.

Haffar: The talk of our lord Nakkar can't' be a lie or pretence. The savior is real. He exists.

Sahm: Exists!!

Haffar: Yes. He exists and is about to manifest himself. Let the teacher tell you about the details.

109

He said this and left ignoring his father who was calling out to him. He headed out leaving his father shocked, the ruler stunned and Sayah supplicating God, "Have mercy on me, O God."

16

Sahm swaggered through the detour, heading toward his dunghill to ponder on things. There was a truth that he heard from the wise hermit and there was the riddle of Nagham which was complicated by a leprous teacher about whom he didn't know too much. His mind was overtaken by 'What-ifs?' along the journey.

What if the leper is honest? What if he is a conspirator? What if the hermit is a liar? What if Nagham doesn't exist? Is there a conspiracy? Does his son realize that there is a conspiracy if there is one? Even his son's talk is nothing but a direct accusation, or rather a threat. What if his son comes back now and there is a proof about his involvement in a fabricated treason by matching his beak prints with those found on the confiscated grains? What if he flies? Will that change the legend of the so-called history?

He was walking slowly, thinking fast with his eyes looking at everything and scanning its details perhaps the subconscious would find a lost truth from a whole world.

Oh my God, help me; help children of hen; save us from the oppressors.

As he was looking at a detour that would lead him to his house, Katkout appeared from nowhere and said, "Sir, I was waiting for you before sunrise."

Sahm: Do you have any news?

Katkout: Actually, I have serious news. There, in the den of the lion, I found your quest. I saw something weird and heard unbelievable things.

Sahm: Talk quickly and continuously.

Katkout: First, I found five white roosters. I thought they were leprous for the teacher was with them, but then I realized that they were from farm chickens, which means that the teacher is one of the intruders. They want to seize the hill farms with the help of the Governor General Abu Rish.

Sahm: It's unbelievable. Why, or rather what's the price?

Katkout: They promised him a big number of servants, and food made of royal grains .Also, they would provide him as well as the males of his own kind with beautiful white hens in return for letting white chickens rule the farm. The strange thing is that they assured him that they would not harm anyone. They even said that they were going to supply all our needs, so that we would remain satisfied and alive.

Sahm: And what is the reason for this generosity? If they had fled from Man, we could have provided them with accommodation and food.

Katkout: No, sir. They talked about many things that I didn't understand at all. They speak a strange language and use human words that they must have learned from human beings. It seems that they are strange beings to our own kind. They are up to no good.

Sahm: What else?

Katkout: I don't know too much about their plans. But when Abu Rish came, they talked in our language. I deduced from their talk that they were planning to fabricate a famine after which they would enter as savior which would make everyone feel grateful for them and accept their presence. And it seems that Abu Rish is the one who would lead them to the hearts of the audience. Hence, I ordered on your behalf the owner of the store to take all the reserve stock to the secret store that only the three of us know about.

It seems that my intuition didn't betray me, Sahm thought. "You did well by hiding the stock," he said to Katkout. "We must play the game backwards, so that their plan would backfire. Go get some rest in the dunghill of the guests located next to the royal one to be ready. I would invite you straight away if need."

Katkout: I'm at your command, sir.

Sahm: Take a different route to the dunghill, so that you could arrive shortly after me. May God protect you.

Katkout: Goodbye.

17

"Where have you been, sir?"

Haffar: I was thinking deeply about myself, perhaps I would find your quest.

Teacher: It's not a quest. It's the truth. Let me be at your service.

Haffar: It's OK, it's OK.

The face of the teacher brightened up at these words and hope was revived in his pursuit again. He started to stare at the face of Haffar studying the birth of his new creature. He tied around his neck the thread of obedience after he had woven the conspiracy attire he was wearing. How poor this Haffar is! He rejoiced over attire on which the savior was written, while it was nothing but an attire of sadness and misery the essence of which was known only by its creator. Seconds of long silence passed the clarity of which was tingled by Haffar's following words, "I studied the article of the assembly of the sages deliberately and couldn't find anyone whose qualities match with those of the savior but me."

Teacher: How honest you are! Were you really looking for someone else? Would you lead us to him if you found him?

Haffar: Certainly. The destiny of the nation is my call and its success is my quest. This matter is serious holding many troubles in it.

Teacher: Do not panic. We all will stand by your side. We will open all doors to you. We will lead you to the savior inside of you. They are hard days forewarning unusual circumstances that need an unusual character. They need you.

Haffar: Your being with me facilitates things and eases hurdles.

Teacher: Let your works talk in the coming days.

Haffar: I can't wait. I actually started to look for the truth.

Teacher: What truth, sir?

Haffar: The truth about the spy bird.

Teacher: The bird is a small truth lost in the threshing floor of the great one. The traitor is a bigger truth that requires firmness to be the key to success in attaining the goal which is the great truth.

Haffar: The great truth! What is it?

Teacher: You're the one who will find it as our lord Nakkar said. Let's wait for the coming days with their sweetness and bitterness.

Haffar: Let it be. Tomorrow is just a day away.

18

The sunset beam reflected on his three-dark stripe golden tail and a royal crest that entailed submissiveness and reverence especially with his long thin beak telling that a prudent was carrying his probe through space to keep his path passablel. His wings spread along the breeze carpet to swagger gently and peacefully piercing with his gaze the farm ground. He saw something that worried him, so he looked here and there in search of an absent friend. Just in a while he took a glimpse of Sahm, so he called out to him at low altitude, "Can you welcome a new friend as old as the walnut tree that you're leaning against, my friend Sahm?"

Sahm: You're most welcome.

Hermit: When I was coming back from the wood, I looked around your farm and saw an unusual hustle and a gathering I'm not used to. Chickens were clustering as if they were up to something. It worried me and my love for you seized me; hence, my curiosity changed into worry and my love was covered by a sadness cloud for fearing for you.

Sahm: Really, the situation is ominous. But before this and that, can I offer you some grains and fresh water?

Zaghloul: It's OK. I need some energy.

The two stood pecking at some grains decorated with pickled worms. Zaghloul liked the taste of pickled worms, so he started to ask about how they were made and preserved. Sahm's answers were dry and incomplete though they were full of politeness and respect.

Zaghloul noticed that, so he asked him, "What's worrying you, my friend?"

Sahm: Don't worry about me, dear.

Zaghloul: It is hard not to worry when I see that you're more anxious than you were the other day? It seems that the situation is worse.

Sahm: It's true my lord, the hermit. It got very complicated. I don't know how and why.

Zaghloul: You stirred my curiosity and awakened sleeping faculties inside of me. Knowing you has affected my being that I loved you; and curiosity increases when it is about someone you love.

Sahm: You put me in a position I would envy myself for. My lord, the hermit...we have been living between that plain and these hills for thousands of years. From time to time we face problems, sometimes from creatures that share this planet with us, sometimes from nature and its disasters. We are used to that; hence, we become ready to be struck by the disaster of this and to be killed by that.

Hermit: We all get used to what we are going through even disasters become our partner in good days. Tell me more, dear.

Sahm: There has been a rise in the number of strangers on this hill especially on my farm over the past few days. Also, talking about coming calamities and a courageous savior who will catch the traitor and reveal the truth has increased.

Zaghloul: Oh my God! What savior and what truth?

Sahm: Even my son started to tempt this and that to leave my farm to join his that some of my wives joined him.

Sahm: Each one of these things is dangerous and harmful to security. So what would happen with all this going on? It couldn't be the coincidence that brought together all this amount of problems. There must be a link, mustn't it?

Sayah: I'm trying to find a reason. We, chicken species, do not harm anyone...or rather we don't know how to do that. We live separately from the rest of the world; we do not fly or travel.

Zaghloul: Did anything that would raise questions happen before the start of the calamities?

Sayah: I don't know anything that would force God to send us a savior. I insist that we're OK and they insist that we're in worse shape. They even started to tight their grip on our sources of food.

Zaghloul: Things took unexpected course. It's not necessary that it is caused by the nature of the problem, but rather because someone is mingling things to look like that. Isn't that what chemists do when they mix some substances together to come up with something different they would claim that they created in front of the ignorant?

Sahm started to think of zaghloul's statement and reflecting upon things. He even was talking to himself from time to time. He did as he pleased in a small yard till Zaghloul heard him saying, "Where are you Nagham? Your presence might lead to our survival and the return of my son to my bosom."

Zaghloul was stunned for a while. Sahm took notice that he overreacted and talked too loud that the hermit heard him. Zaghloul looked at him with scrutinizing eyes and said, "Did it happen that someone called you Sayah??"

Sahm was stunned. He was overtaken by surprise for no one knew this name but her. Certainly the hermit had nonpareil skills. Still, could he see the unseen? His surprise intensified as long seconds passed. But Zaghloul broke the silence and asked, "You haven't answered my question, yet. You didn't even ask me how I guessed your name...don't you want to know?"

Sahm: Yes, I'm Sayah and no one knows this name but a bird. Please don't confuse me!

Zaghloul: Or rather you don't know anyone but her, do you? Her description of your physical appearance and personality was accurate, and that is why I estimated that it was you for long time, but I didn't want to say anything before now.

Sayah: Woe is me! Did she tell you all this before she died?

Zaghloul: Hold on! Who said she died? She is alive and kicking. She is doing great.

Sayah: Is that possible after all that happened. I blamed myself too much. Just a few days ago I knew that she was on the brink of death; that she was subject to torture and humiliation and that she disappeared mysteriously.

Zaghloul : Yes, everything you don't know is mysterious.

Sayah: But how did she survive?

Zaghloul: God always helps his oppressed people. Yes, there are grudge and hatred. There are also machinations and conspiracies for the sake of power and usually innocent people are the ones who would pay dearly for it. Isn't a shame that the cost of material power tarnished all spiritual principles?

Sayah: So, she endured great suffering from dirty beaks, or rather wicked souls.

Zaghloul: Yes, but your God was there for her. The one, whom God stands by, cannot be harmed by anyone's intrigue.

Sayah: You figured out long time ago how miserable I am in her absence! Why didn't you cheer me up or rather why didn't Nagham contact me, then?

Zaghloul: It is not about consolation. For what I know is not mine and have no right to disclose it. But I found a way to get through what I know to you when you mentioned her, so I liked to shower you with her memory.

Sayah brightened up as he didn't for so long. He fluttered a little bit and started to run around Zaghloul with joy and cheerfulness.

"She is okay, then. Where is she or rather how did she survive? How did you find her? Please tell me, tell me everything," he said to him.

Happiness was written all over the face of the hermit who was glad that Sahm was happy after the disaster that was inflected upon him. To not waste excitement time and stop the storm of joy that blew their beings away, he said, "One day of last autumn a patient visited me looking for a medication that wasn't available in the corners of my tree house. Among what I wanted was a rare herb that I am planting at a bushy basil trunk in the forest of the basil near your kingdom. I arrived after dawn. A low moan attracted me, so I got closer to see ruins and many broken branches. I got closer toward the moan to find delicacy and beauty fighting death and life; a delicate bird stained with blood. Yes, some wanted to prove that their opinion is right, and to prove their opinion, they insisted on backing it up with the blood of the living.

"It doesn't matter whose blood would be. Yes, we must shed our blood to obtain our freedom and that of our own kind. And it seems that some think that they must shed innocent people's blood to enjoy power along with privileges they called freedom; a freedom pertaining to their highness. Yes, some wanted to bury mercy, silence the song and love little by little, so that its moan would become pleasant to their ears.

"Sometimes, tormented voices would impart ecstasy of victory to some creatures and kill the remnants of the conscience in them. They are the most successful ways of enslaving others once they give in."

Tears fell down from the sky... and terror fell on the busted heart that it was about to break. But his knowing that she was alive warmed his heart.

"What a crime! Go ahead sir, your story is sad and painful and your presence there in the midst of terror moments would make leaves fall off the sorrow tree," he said.

Zaghloul added, "I gathered from the wood what I thought would help her to recover. I and a passing bird took her to my tree house. I was worried about her so much for her wound was torn open with a savagery showing that the doer had too much of spite and grudge in him apart from the filthiness of their beaks and the ground's dirtiness. In the beginning she lost a lot of blood and weight, but God's care saved her. There is something weird I noticed about her. It was that smile adorning her face with a lot of hope. It was always there and still, yes, it didn't dim. When I saw you, I knew that there was a body for that picture overwhelming her face. She loves you."

Sayah: How generous you are, God! I live just to see her, to take here where she wants and makes her happy as she pleases. Her disappearance made me confused and stripped smile from my house. But my heart hasn't throbbed with another name but hers since I met her. Oh, how is she doing now? Where is she?

Zaghloul: She improved over time and learned a lot about the life of hermits. An old hermit helped her mediate and perceive things differently. Her pure and spotless soul got brighter and more sparkling with meditation and worship.

Sayah: Did she become a hermit thus giving up her share of worldly life.

Zaghloul: Don't panic! Hermits are ordinary creatures who look at things and see in them a glimpse of God's face. Also, whenever she did something, she did it to seek God's pleasure.

Sayah: Please, show me the way to her.

Zaghloul: All in good time. As for now, tell me what you were hiding from me for fear of misunderstanding, or perhaps for believing that I would not understand what you are going through.

The two talked a lot for long time. Sayah told him his story with Nagham and the arriving white chickens. The hermit kept silent for too long and tried to link threads together in his mind perhaps he would understand the sentence attire that this farm or at least Sayah would wear.

No, no he must solve those riddles and cut these threads, but how? It doesn't matter how because there is always a means to triumph over evil. Isn't supporting the oppressed and mangling the intrigue of the oppressors what God committed himself to do?

The strength of the faith of Zaghloul was crystallize in his words to Sayah, " You have to be alert and gather around you those who are loyal to you among your own kind and rely on them even a little bit, my friend Sayah. Also be aware of the ignorant for an ignorant friend would harm you more than a well-informed enemy. Rely on God and let your belief in winning be certain because God doesn't accept a partner."

Sayah: Thanks, my friend, the hermit.

Zaghloul: We must keep in touch in these hard circumstances. I want you to know that my tree house is opened for you anytime especially if you are in imminent danger.

19

Three roosters were standing in a deserted hen-house looking at each other wrapped in silence as if they were strangers. One of them was chewing thoughts in his beak to put them in his head that was rejecting them because they weren't chewed very well. Still, he was trying over and over to understand the essence of this meeting that was attended by a rooster he could barely remember in his mind which developed in the bosom of nature.

There was no room for dreams or grudges in his heart. Yes, every rooster grew up to come to power because his behavior and make-up imposed on him that. He received attention and training more than anyone else as his father took great care of him and provided him with affection and experience more than his friends for he came from a glorious home.

But germs of new feelings infiltrated him mentally and physically; hence, they started to take control of him little by little. But the source of the pandemic would not stop until it caught his body in the same way as fire would catch straw from every side. His pride and grandeur saturated with germs of spite pushed him to ask, "Did the teacher invite me to tell me that it's time to show up as I am?" But he didn't wait for an answer from anyone but himself.

Yes, what made him meet me in this isolated place is to receive a preferential treatment. My satisfaction is significant. Tomorrow, everyone will know that I'm the savior. Tomorrow I will make them happy and give them a decent life. I will kill the spy bird and find the traitor. Hold on! How would I find him... and who is he? The talk of the teacher about my father isn't true for I find out that apart from loving us, my father loved chickens, all chickens. What's the rush? Didn't our lord Nakkar say that the savior will do so? Hold on! Who's that third rooster?

The other rooster was walking back and forth. This poor rooster will realize now that his father is involved and even guilty, he thought. The halo would fall off the ruler and his son's heart will be terrified by that. He might cry or run away from his self or perhaps would kill me. O my God! That might happen. He might kill me to bury the secret out of fear of scandal and shame. But I came here against my will. I'm greatly indebted to my lord Sahm, and didn't want to be the one who would tell his son, my lord Haffar. But I'm just an employee that knows but little and if my job hadn't been pertaining to print identification, I wouldn't have been forced to do that. Maybe my lord Abu Rish, wanted me to tell his son in the hope of finding a way out. Have mercy on me, O God.

As for the third rooster, it was the teacher. The teacher wanted silence to shake trust and leave the one who was lost bewildered, perhaps that would make the prey easy to catch. He knew his prey very well. He stood for long with stray wandering eyes that every pupil strayed in a side which the other pupil cannot reach. All of a sudden, he turned to the print examiner and said, "We came here under the command of Abu Rish, the chief, for a special mission, Inspector.

The Inspector nodded his head and said, "Yes, we came here secretly just to preserve the dignity of this honored young master. This is what our lord Abu Rish wanted, because the family of this rooster is one of the most glorious families on the hill and he is even the descendant of our lord Nakkar. No one else but the three of us will know what's going on here."

Haffar was stunned by these riddles. He said, "Get to the heart of the mater, teacher. Do not be afraid of anything."

The teacher looked at the third rooster and said, "Tell us, Inspector, in a totally scientific way about the results of your analysis."

Inspector: For more than a year, I have been working to match the prints found on the confiscated grains in the accident of the spy bird with any rooster or hen. But I couldn't find anything. A few days ago my lord Abu Rish ordered me to look into the records of those who are granted immunity. After searching, I found that there is a match with...

The inspector fell silent as if words evaporated from his mouth all of a sudden that Haffar yelled at his face, "Tell me who he is!"

Inspector: Please, spare me.

Teacher: We don't have time for emotions for we all know how faithful you are.

The inspector hesitated and then said quickly, "They are the prints of my lord Sahm."

Haffar: Woe is me. This is what I was worried about.

Teacher: Thank you, Inspector. You can dismiss now.

With eyes softened and the crest down, the teacher gave Haffar a look for which he made a body from compassion and from mercy a veil and then said, "O son, I didn't want to tell you the truth to hate your father ,but rather to realize a truth that might support you. On top of that these are but the orders of my lord Abu Rish."

Haffar: It's the truth I fear. How would I rejoice over it when it affects my core?

Teacher: The truth of things is not what it seems when you delve into it. This incidence might incriminate your father, but who knows? It might hold in it good.

Haffar: How is that? Doesn't this truth mean clearly that my father is the traitor? How can I be the savior and my father is a traitor... Didn't I tell you that I'm not the savior?

Teacher: The virtuous are always tested by God through their loved ones. Also, you have to make sure of that and if, God forbid, it happened and you were certain of this bitter truth, everyone will highly respect you. Everyone will realize that you're so faithful that you are sacrificing your father for the sake of the truth that everyone was looking for.

Haffar: How would I face my own kind and I know the truth about my father's being involved in something that signs and even conclusive evidence point out.

Teacher: Perhaps my lord, Sahm, is unknowingly involved. And perhaps he was lured by the bird into treason trap.

Haffar: My father is too intelligent to fall prey to her.

Teacher: You know your father better than anyone else. But you're the hope. That's what we're looking for, and even that's what we know. You have to do what a savior has to do. Follow your conscience, perhaps you would find a way to save face.

Haffar: What do you mean?

Teacher: You can move your father away to a place where he cannot get this nation involved in something that would harm it and we would keep this a secret. I don't think that my lord Abu Rish would mind for the goal here is to save the nation not to take revenge on him.

Haffar: Perhaps...perhaps. Everything is possible in this hard time.

Teacher: let things happen naturally perhaps you would find a way out that would please you. And what I said was just a thought. Still, let's us remember that our lord Nakkar said it's you who would kill the bird and catch the traitor.

Haffar: Here you are saying a traitor.

Teacher: Excuse me sir. It is a slip of tongue. Perhaps my lord Sahm would lead us to the traitor.

Haffar: This slip of tongue expresses a truth that you fear to reveal for me.

The teacher: Excuse me, sir. It is you who is going to tell us the truth.

Haffar: Perhaps I have to face my farther with that...I will find the right time to do so.

The teacher's face brightened up at this good piece of news and his heart laughed.

You're not going to catch up with the right time, he thought. Things will go faster than your thinking.

133

Then he looked at Haffar and said, "Be careful, sir, and do not hesitate to invite me whenever you want.

20

The next day, on the rule dunghill, Abu Rish was walking back and forth as the teacher and two roosters of Abu Rish's assistants were watching him. Abu Rish was brusque and the tremble of his feathers, the redness of his crest with the mixture of the whiteness of his eyes made him harsher that he would disgust anyone who saw him.

That was worrying and stressful to the attendees who were waiting for something obscure. All of a sudden, he looked with his left eye to the teacher and said, "Where is the chief? Isn't he supposed to be here now?"

The teacher answered him with fear decorated with official attributes, "I'm sure he is on his way. As you know, he must be careful in these circumstances."

"I know, I know. It's all right," Abu Rish said.

Just a few minutes later, the chief showed. He looked tired. He said, "What's the matter, my lords? You worried me."

Abu Rish: The plan will be ruined. Sahm informed me that the reserve stock of grains was stolen from stores and this includes the food of the ten farms on this hill. We will be in big trouble if the daily supplies stop.

Chief: How is that possible? How could stores be stolen especially now?

Abu Rish: Weren't we going to hide the stock, and then supply them with food little by little on the grounds that you're a good neighbor. How is it possible that the stock was stolen now and wasn't before at all? Is it a mere coincidence?

The chief said, "How stupid you are? There is no room for coincidence in the life of nations. I bet there is someone who hid among trees and eavesdropped on us. Who would do such a thing? I will take care of this later. Still, the disappearance of food or stealing it is worrying me and we have to think profoundly why the food was stolen the time we were going to hide it! Did the news leak out? Who did this? Where was Sahm in the past days? Who was he meeting and where? Shouldn't there be someone who follows him wherever he may go?" he said that as he was looking at the teacher and Abu Rish and then he asked them, "Isn't it the responsibility of both of you?!" The two looked stunned but they didn't reply.

Abu Rish looked at the chief and said, "Of course, we will do. There will be a tight control from now on. But why do we hurry to accelerate the operation? Chickens are here and they won't go anywhere as they haven't done since forever."

The chief answered angrily, "First, you should have watched Sahm once you knew that he found out about the matter of the bird and since he started to inquire about the matter and its reasons. Second, you crossed the line for we agreed that execution would be your responsibility and guidance would be ours. As for now, we have to keep a tight grip on food, so that everyone would feel the taste of hunger. After that, faces would be owned by the one who would put a grain of wheat in their mouths."

The chief fell silent a bit and then nodded to the teacher to follow him to one of the corner. He told him, "Why didn't you keep me updated with what happened with our promising savior?"

Teacher: I beg your pardon. It was too late when we finished and when Abu Rish kept me posted about this disaster for which we came here. But do not worry for he is at our beck and call.

Chief: We should not let him think. Let the pace of things be fast. You have to bridle and prepare him to be released at H hour. And do not forget to spit out your poisons in your acquaintances that it is time for the savior to come out from his long hibernation to help children of hen, and that they must be patient and ready to support him.

The chief and the teacher went back to the ring of conversation where the chief took charge. He said, "I want you immediately to start a media campaign to the effect that there is a traitor who sold his own kind and stole the food of his own species. Let the accusation be obscure till you receive other instructions in this regard."

The meeting was over and each went in a different direction. Katkout withdrew gently from his hiding place and headed quickly to the dunghill of Sahm to tell him how things turned out because of the conspiracy of his own kind against him.

The story about the savior was the main concern and today the story about food took a turn for the worse. He knew the story about food and Katkout acted in a way that would save the farm from starvation for a short period of time.

As for this savior, what's his story? Who is he or rather where is he? And how did this savior fall from the sky?

They talked transparently to get to the heart of the matter, to find out what the goal of white chickens could be and why they wanted to conquer these farms and keep them under their control.

Is it really that Abu Rish is going to give up on his glory for some white hens? What do these comers want from farms of children of Adam? and what about their talk that resembles that of children of Adam as Katkout said? Sayah thought. Katkout is intelligent and honest. His talk matches with the hints of the teacher and my son Haffar. O God, they are hard days that need the wisdom of our lord Nakkar -He sighed deeply - and to the presence of Nagham.

After a long time he felt like eternity, he said to Katkout, "I'm going to the hermitage and hide for a few days. No one should know my place. You and the grain storekeeper must distribute grains at the highest level of confidentiality. Do not attract the attention of anyone especially that of the followers of Abu Rish. I hope that I come back soon with a solution that would save us from this corrupt clique. You alone know my place, so do not come to me unless there is a disaster. The life of the nation is precious and the truth is one of the keys to knowledge and knowledge is freedom...I am leaving for the sake of the key."

21

Sayah arrived at the origin of the willow tree. He crowed with determination and sorrow over and over. He waited and waited moments he felt like eternity. All of a sudden, a bird perched beside him and greeted him in a soft voice. Confusion overtook him for a while, and then increased when he saw something descending from the back of the hoopoe to appear all of a sudden the most beautiful picture he had ever seen. It was Nagham…yes, Nagham.

"Oh my God, how gracious you are!" Sayah said.

"Hello darling Sayah. My longing was more powerful than my ability to wait," Nagham said.

"How happy I am with the union of lovers. I will go back to my tree house," Zaghloul said.

"No, sir, your reverence is too dignified to not equate to the love that is overwhelming us."

"Wisdom is still tickling this beautiful head...your presence warmed my heart," Nagham said.

"Were you here during my last visit?" Sayah said.

"Yes. I heard all your talk, but I took control of my heart not to ruin your decisions about ruling. It seemed to me the other day that you were in need for the wisdom of our lord more than love and its dreams," she replied.

"They might equate or perhaps love would prevail. Still, responsibility imposes on us to let go of our feelings...events are moving fast," he said.

Zaghloul interfered, stunned, "Is there something new?"

"Grudges overtook us that a slave started to compete against his lord for a throne that he has never dreamed of seeing," Sayah answered him.

Both said at once, "Oh my God... what happened and how?"

"A group of white chickens, chickens of children of Adam farms, act in an unusually intelligent, shrewd way and want to take control of our potentials for an unknown reason. The start we know was a year ago when they hurt Nagham and conspired against her. They are about to accuse me of high treason by proving truth with bad intent. You know the truth about the grains that I brought to Nagham to recover. Those became the crime tool."

"Hold on! You have to know the truth," Zaghloul said.

Sayah: The truth...the truth...perhaps the so-called savior would find it.

"The savior? Is he a new creature?" Nagham said in a sad surprised voice.

Sayah: It's a long, interesting story...it could even be fatal.

"But everything lies in knowing the truth. When truth comes out, we will realize how kind-hearted we are. Sometimes we don't differentiate between kindness and stupidity. Still, finding the truth takes honesty, courage...and sacrifice."

Sayah: This is what I'm looking for. But it seems that the path of truth is full of pains and sacrifices and there is someone who will pay dearly for it...I wish it would me.

He stopped talking for a while, then added, "Excuse me I was overtaken by the beautiful surprise that I didn't ask Nagham about her inability to fly."

"It's a cheap price for staying alive in the care of this hermit and carrying on my life to see you again. Yes, it's a permanent disability resulting from the assault," Nagham answered.

Sayah was stunned by the reality that didn't cross his mind, but noticed that Nagham continued to say, "A reasonable creature would understand his submissive powers when the obvious ones collapse, so he would build an edifice in himself, more dignified and more sublime."

A moments of meditation reigned before Zaghloul would say, "Let's go to the tree house to delve into this issue" -he looked at Sayah- "I will take Nagham and then will drop by."

The tree house was shielded by the leaves of the pointed willow tree which Zaghloul arranged in an intelligent way and God blessed with his protection, so that he would remain a source of wisdom in the world of birds. Wasn't wisdom a blessed unknown gift in loyal hearts that would only appear in hard days?

Sayah was surprised at the vastness of the place for he feared that his size would be an obstacle or would cause his host embarrassment. Zaghloul understood the situation of Sayah, so he reminded him that the place was for all birds, those that could fly and those that couldn't, and that's why the place had to be spacious.

The hermit looked at Sayah and told him, "You won't be able to think properly unless you empty the disasters of this small head into oblivion quiver and get a physical and mental rest. Close your eyes, let your imagination float along nothingness lake, allow your flaws to decompose little by little to become part of it and go into deep sleep till your subconscious finds its path toward purity and urges you to meet it in reality. You will know your goal and know where to start, then."

The hermit's words found their way into Sayah's ears little by little until he understood what Zaghloul said. Then he crept to a calm corner and lulled his senses into a deep sleep.

After a long time he didn't know how long it was, he came back from where he was to find the shade and the spirit of Nagham watching over him and protecting him like willow's leaves and stars of Milky Way galaxy. Also, the spirit of the hermit was overwhelming him with wisdom fragrance and knowledge incense to be his spell protecting him from being the victim of the slaughterhouse of the souls competing to seize control of what's not theirs and to take what they didn't own.

He wanted to start over, so he narrated his story again. They discussed it and put all possibilities according to their knowledge of the facts of the other side. Sayah heard from Nagham her tragedy with her sweet voice. His loving heart softened and her longing bird fluttered around him. After deliberations in the case of chickens ranging from the confiscated grains to the unknown savior, Nagham looked at Sayah with wondering eyes and told him, "It seems that you are hiding something."

"Yes, I wanted to clarify my mind to take a decision and I haven't yet. The matters that need urgent decision started to keep me awake and I don't know how things ended up in my home. And to be more effective and right, I want your help together with that of my lord the hermit to face my harsh circumstances."

"Go ahead sir, Governor," she said it with the coquetry of a beloved and the confidence of a prudent. "We talked and discussed the case of white chickens. The matter of grains that were in your possession is something vulnerable. I can tell them the truth, but do they have the willingness to believe? Really, I want to hear your opinion about the story of the savior and the matter of flying which you undoubtedly heard my discussion over it with my lord the hermit," Sayah said.

"First, there is a missing thread about what they want from you or from your own kind, but it seems that there is a great benefit behind their intrigue. Your remark about their extreme intelligence leads us to one of two things: they are either mercenary falling under the spell of son of Adam or they really developed into another creature," she said. "It is an interesting analysis. Go ahead please," Sayah said.

Nagham continued to speak, "This is what I'm going to build my thinking on in the coming hours. And till things in the world of truth would decompose, I will reflect upon facts from different angles perhaps I would find a solution that would lead us to what we're looking for with fewer losses. As for the matter of the savior, it's the weirdest thing we have ever heard. My lord the hermit tells me that your life has been tedious since the beginning of time, so why would he come now? Isn't it a riddle? What would he save you from? Is there an ordeal inflected upon you that you need to be saved from?"

"As you said nothing new has come up for thousands of years except for our story. Also, they don't know anything about the truth. They found a body of a ewe and dressed it in a lion's fur...and then felt scared of it and wove stories about their heroisms with the lion lurking in the unknown." Sayah said.

Nagham: So, all that we have to do is find the missing ring to complete the necklace of the truth.

Sayah :I want that necklace at any cost to put it around your necklace the day of our wedding.

146

Nagham : You're making me blush... let's change the subject. I will leave the topic about flying for Zaghloul for I feel embarrassed. I said about you things that I didn't mean and I might have done this before feeling something for you.

Zaghloul came and listened to them ... his gazes lingered on the eyes of the attendees and then his gazes unfathomed those of Sayah. Afterward he asked, "Do you want the truth without equivocation?"

"Yes, it's the most dignified thing I'm looking for," Sayah said with eagerness and longing.

Zaghloul looked at him and said, "The most beautiful painting that time draws is that of mere truth. It's universe beauty in civilization painting that you can see yourself only if you're part of it."

He fell silent a while, and then added, "I thought that the world of chickens and their partners forgot or pretended to forget the matter of flying. And even each has their own world since an age that even our ancestors did not witness. But I see that bubbles of questions and rumors floating along the lake of your life again on your small farms.

"The reason doesn't matter for the problem is serious. I am afraid that it would get more serious and overtake the calmness of your life. I fear for you because of its distress and sorrow .The tree of spite and grudge would not yield but destruction."

Sayah was stunned by the bitter reality that the shrewdness of this dignified bird can seize. He said with pain and sadness, "I thought it is dangerous, but you depict it as destruction."

There was in the gazes of Zaghloul a sufficient answer, but he wanted to explain further to his interrogator, so he said, "There is a truth with bad intent. This matter didn't occupy your mind before you met Nagham. The harsh words of Nagham were the first indication of the flow of ambition that overwhelmed you. But you could find a way out of your embarrassment in front of your beloved only after the appearance of the first teacher in your life who blew life in a thousand-year-old dead person. He unveiled the curtain off a mummy that was nesting inside of you. The white chickens lit the

147

fuse to get something we don't know and I don't think that he will leave before attaining his goal. I think that he is but a messenger of evil; of a Satan that is bigger and more powerful than him."

"What shall we do? Isn't there a way?"

Questions overwhelmed the feathers of Sayah. His beak revealed what was going through him as if the wound unfathomed the spot of the pain; hence, silence reigned in the place that even the wind could not break through it. After a long time that was moments in time counter, Zaghloul said, "There is one way to get you out of this. You are on the brink of a painful end."

Sayah: Help me, sir. Tell me what I have to do.

Zaghloul : There is nothing to do. There is a reference to the origin of the issue and I think that the white chickens are using that for some reason. Also, I think that what inside of you equates with the other half of the problem because personal influence determines the level of a person's willingness to sacrifice and to take risks. As long as the personal dream matches with that of the group, the individual would desire additional giving to end with absolute giving. For this reason, you have to fly.

Sayah: Fly! Oh my God, how or rather why?

Zaghloul: Take it easy and listen. The matter is deeply rooted in your history and civilization. Even the terror you feel and your fright from flying is the outcome of an ordeal that your grandfather Nakkar went through because of his companions together with your twisted history that you inherited. What they call a mark of shame because of a fake document can change into success and power if you can fly. A new world is waiting for you, so are you going to enter it or not?

Sayah seemed stunned. He thought of flying many times just for seconds or for fraction of a second and every time the idea was totally rejected. He rather denied it before posing the question. And now Zaghloul was asking from him to fly. It was a disaster that Nagham lifted him from its bottom when she said, "Undoubtedly, he will think deeply and clearly without a delay realizing that we are by his side to the end."

Sayah: Alright. I will do that. As for now my lord the hermit would you please tell us what you think about the so-called savior.

Zaghloul: We haven't heard about your savior before. I don't have any knowledge about this matter either. Still, what I'm sure about is that disasters might be followed by a savior or other outcomes. But that a savior would come out and wait for a disaster to save is something unbelievable. And what's strange is that your savior told you or almost did about the time of his arrival. So, are you going to see him first or see what you're afraid of? However, the big question is, 'Who is the savior?' And the bigger question is, 'Do you need him?'

149

22

The amount of available grains started to decrease gradually as the chief had imposed a tough blockade on the farm to create the reality he wanted. Also, Katkout was not generous in distribution. The provisions would never arrive when needed too besides the fact that they would not satisfy the needs of individuals because the guards of Abu Arish were everywhere. His mission got harder.

The amount of eggs started to decrease; the curtain of death began to fall on chicks; the cluck of hens became moans; the sky over that hill was sad, and asking about Sahm who went on a special mission, as his associates said, increased. The pressures on chickens' community got tighter, so that the time of weakness would come and they would accept whoever came as a savior. The savor was getting ready fast.

There was talk here and there about the dire condition that the farm ended up to. Rays of hopes that the prophecy of our lord Nakkar would become a reality, started to infiltrate through the fences of hen-houses as well. "What prophecy?" the dormant wondered. "The time approached when the savoir would appear," the voice of night guards answered.

"Save us from what?" the dormant said.

"From what we're going through," the bats of darkness said.

The hungry and scared mouths sighed, saying, "No, we don't want to be saved. We want food and safety."

"Traitors will be killed and food will be sent," the ghosts whispered closer.

"Tell us when he comes," the dreamers said.

"Stay still in your beds and pray that God may bless his deeds," the insinuation of the guards hid in their ears.

"Amen," everyone said.

"Take this food from the savior and vow him on victory," the night caller said.

The crowd took the food, went to sleep and said, "We promise him." They all lost the hope for a prompt solution and realized that famine was caused by a traitor who sold his country. They wanted to kill that traitor and banish him from their home and embrace that savior perhaps he would be a cure.

The aids of the savior arrived secretly with an oath of allegiance. The hungry would pledge to allegiance, the scared would pledge to allegiance, and the lost would pledge to allegiance. But the chickens that were used to living in the crucible of their cowardice would never think of how to obtain things. They might be even forced not to think for generations and they were used to being a victim as it was said.

But the victim of what? This was the question. Just a few roosters were ruling and taking charge of everything. And taking any decision depended only on them. The rest kept clucking, while the males kept crowing and then would return by evening to the same dunghill that they inherited over hundreds of years to sleep with their simplicity and cowardice. They would just complain about scarcity of food and the vastness of the place. But the devil sent those that would urge children of hen to promise victory to the savior when his star would appear through darkness. He who doused the light of the sun, wanted to light for them a candle. How ironic! Some of us could not see the bright sun, while they would dance out of happiness with a candle whose light would illuminate no more than one stumbling step. The truth was a scary thing in the minds of the cowards.

Katkout and some of Sahm's associates who bore for him a special loyalty were comforting people that Sahm went on a special mission to solve the simple problem of food and the serious one of the nation. No one asked about this or that because their trust in Sahm was bigger than hunger or perhaps because they didn't distinguish between this and that. There was always a group of elite that would carry on its shoulder the hope of the nation. But the leprous teacher was spreading secretly among his followers that Sayah would not return because he stole the grains and immigrated to another hill to start a new life. Days passed. They were as bad as the previous ones; the production of eggs started to decline and the supply of the grains that Katkout saved was almost as flat as the ground.

In the den of the lion, the chief convened with the best of his assistants including the leprous teacher. The chief asked about the news of Sahm, so the teacher said, "Our spies are watching every place, but there is no trace of him. And we noticed that he has an employee named Katkout who distributes food to some members of the farm secretly. It seems that he is involved in the disappearance of the supply of the grains."

Chief: Do not arrest him. Keep a close eye on him to be our guide to Sahm's hiding place.

Teacher: Of course, sir. I'm sure that he will lead us to Sahm so soon.

Chief: We don't have too much time. We must move to another stage.

Abu Kamha: Don't you think that waiting for some time would be beneficial to us, sir? Chief: No, dear. We must hurry up because there are thousands of farm chickens that need elevation before it's too late.

Abu Kamha: Let us intensify the blockade until they perish and then we colonize the whole hill. It is sufficient to chickens from all farms.

Chief: We need these chickens to execute our scheme. Our grandchildren would end up like our ancestors.

Abu Kamha: Excuse me, sir, would you please explain the matter further, so that we could understand its importance.

Chief: I like your questions, but it's not the suitable time for that...and if I die, you would find in my will what suits you. As for now, let us move to the next phase through which we look forward to being accepted by chickens as their rulers. Teacher: We must humiliate and frighten them, so that they would find in us their salvation.

Chief: Sadly, this is true and it is astonishing how chickens, though cowardly and submissive, consider themselves to be superior to us and treat us with disdain. This era must come to an end so soon.

"Let us decide the steps of execution," the chief said as he was signaling to the guards to go away.

23

Zaghloul and Nagham stood giving their instructions and advice to Sayah that was not only convinced but also determined to fly. He started to tame, soften his body and strengthen his muscles as the instructions of Nisr Abu Al-Makhaleb stated in the guarded tablets.

Zaghloul edited them, so they would suit the knowledge he had acquired over thousands of years. Sayah would stand, curse and insult. Sometimes despair would overwhelm him and the bad companion would convince him to run away even from himself. But the heart of his beloved and the prayer of the hermit were the healing cure for the wounds of the tough time. As time passed, he started to feel that he had two wings that were working more than they used to be in his entire life. He would begin to fly some meters and then would fall on his head or belly. A laugh hid pain, another expressed the joy of making progress along with a withering smile showing fear for the poor creature in him was still lurking in him. It was hard for him to smother a friend lurking inside of him teaching him fear and cowardice; that creature that chickens inherited from their ancestors, a legacy that could not be declined.

At last he flew higher than the tree house and further than the third three. He fell on the ground and crowed too much and his crow expressed his joy that was equated with Nagham's chirps and Zaghloul's prayers. He yelled, "I can fly. I must go home today. Yes, today."

But Nagham told him, "Oh my darling, you have just started. You must stay for a while to master flying. Your success foretokens a new world and a defeat of intruders by revealing the truth."

Katkout reached the hermitage exhausted. He told his lord Sahm, about what happened, "The rumor said that you stole the supply and that you're cooperating with the enemy. What happened yesterday was extremely horrifying."

Sahm: What happened?

Katkout: We found two murdered hens in the square of the village. Their feathers were plucked and their eyes were gouged out. The scene was very appalling.

Sahm: Who did that? Who dared to do that?

Katkout: Please, sir, come home quickly for there are a lot of pressures on your supporters and the supply of food is running out quickly, or rather we don't have enough food to eat. The grip of Abu Rish is getting tighter.

Sahm: Tell everyone that I'm coming home in a few days .Our history will then change for the better forever."

Katkout was stunned and silent.

Sahm: I know how hard it is. Tell my supporters to remain strong for just a few days.

Katkout: Your supporters are getting scarce like the rare food. Yes, many of your supporters dismounted the vehicle of your rule and rode another train that hasn't come yet.

Sahm: What do you mean?

Katkout: Everyone is waiting for that so-called savior.

Sahm: I know about the savior and how dangerous he is, but I have to return with the cure not with blandishment.

"I beg your pardon, sir. You don't know what happened to us. They are the worst days in the history of the farm since it came into existence. They won't believe the story of your return that lingered in a tough circumstance .Their hearts are with you but their bodies are loyal to the one who fills their beaks. Hunger is unfaithful. You have to choose between the fire of homecoming and the hell of waiting."

Sahm: Woe to you! Choose what?

Katkout : I beg your pardon once again, sir. I mean choosing between hiding from enemies' spies and fighting. I fear that they would ravish our hens and steal our pride. The one who took chickens' lives yesterday wants to humiliate us. Doing that means he doesn't fear God, so how would he fear us, then?

Sahm: What a calamity! Nothing can keep he who violates morals and walks out on virtues away from committing vices. But everything has a cost. Truth will rise for pains and scapegoats that we pay are nothing but the advance we pay for a decent life. I will return soon with a victory banner coming from the sky. Don't ask me how and why. Just go back with your head held high.

158

Katkout : I don't doubt any word you said. I don't doubt your love for us either...but oppression and hunger are the work of the devil. I beg your pardon. See you soon.

24

A white rooster entered the dunghill of roosters' gathering where a special meeting was held to assess things.

"I brought you certain news, sir," he told the chief.

Chief: It seems that you knew his whereabouts.

Rooster: Yes, sir. Your intuition was right. At last Katkout went in disguise to the hiding place of his majesty Sahm. He is in the remote hermitage hosted by hermit Zaghloul.

Chief: Tell me what you saw and heard in details.

Rooster: I couldn't hear anything for the place was vast. But I saw a hoopoe. I think it was the hermit in the company of a small bird I couldn't see clearly.

Chief: Thank you. You can sit outside till I send for you again.

After the exit of the guard the chief said, "We found Sahm through his threads. Let's start to cut his threads one by one and carry on with the second phase while we prepare for the third one which is celebrating the anniversary of our lord Nakkar after a week."

Abu Kamha: What do you mean? What is his anniversary, sir? We haven't done this before!

Chief: Really, we must start something new that would link the world of chickens to one centre. Since the life story of our lord Nakkar was the essence of children's meeting, we must revive it in the world of grown-ups as well. Let them feel regret for things no one but them have done for years and let's them weep over he who died happy. Twist and change whatever you want as long as the core of the case is subjugating this farm and even all farms for our new world. You must mention all perils and make them look more horrifying. Afterwards, promise them that the savior is absolutely coming.

Teacher: Is it time, sir?

Chief: You and he must be ready.

Teacher: There is an army of white chickens waiting for the savior to be at his disposal. They would promise that.

Abu Kamha: And what's next?

Chief: We strike.

Abu Kamha: Excuse me, sir. Can't you see that we're going to take many lives and that we might ruin the farm? We all feel grateful to you. We became smarter and more powerful, but does that give us the right to kill especially that we don't see any reason to do that except for complying with your orders and those of your leadership.

Chief: I'm glad you asked. I was going to explain myself once this phase was over, but it's OK, I'm going to tell you. I was born in one of the incubators in the world of son of Adam and I was raised on his farm. It just happened that one of rich kids bought me to be an entertaining toy. But he was luxurious, so he gave up on me after a few days. They put me on a small farm that included colored chickens, but the colored chickens disdained me and banished me to the end of the farm without food and water. I lived on the top of their dung and I had to poke here and there to look for food. And it just happened that I found a type of mushrooms that grew only at their dung, so I started to feed on it.

After a while, I found myself capable of understanding and analyzing things; hence, the small farm chickens appeared to be stupid. I realized after a short time that I could hear and understand. I knew that it was called intelligence and that intelligence was what distinguished creatures whose ruler was the most intelligent of them not the most powerful.

I started to observe Man, listen to him and learn from him. I tried that type of mushrooms on some hens. Some died; others lost their mind till I found the right recipe. Ironically, this type of mushrooms grows only under the dung of colored chickens and we should use it in a particular case and at a particular age. For this reason, we must remain here as masters taking control of the quality and type of mushrooms. It's our duty to save the farm chickens from children of Adam.

Everyone was surprised at what they heard and at the fact that they were nothing but the outcome of the hard work of the chief. But Abu Kamha wondered if there was a moral reason to enslave the farm members and leave them to perish. This depended on the ethics of the new generation. But he did not dare to reveal what it was going on inside of him.

As days passed, the amount of grains available on the farms of the hill decreased, or rather disappeared. The mission of Katkout to distribute food to Sahm's supporters, whose numbers shrank like food, got harder and harder because guards were everywhere. The farm was divided into three divisions: a division that kept staying alive with the small amount of grains that it received from Katkout; a division to which food was sent as a reward for waiting for the savior. As for the biggest division, it received nothing. The chief decided to be tough on them rather than kill them. For this reason, the tragedy was harder on Sahm's supporters and those who were partial.

The quantity of eggs decreased, many chicks died, the atmosphere got dreary, and the question about Sahm and the reason behind his long absence increased. Those that spread rumors started to spit their poisons claiming that Sahm escaped with the money of stolen food, that he was involved in the case of the spy and her dirty world and that the savior would inevitably appear.

With every new dawn break, one could hardly hear roosters' crow over the high hills. Enthusiasm was dimmed, bodies became thin and voices started to look like crying...a powerless voice; a discontinuous crow with a string of sobbing in it. While one of the roosters was looking out upon the farm yard from a high place, he noticed that a big number of hens died from starvation between the alleys. He was still under shock, when he heard the chief of hens wailing and screaming, "Five laying hens were found killed with their feathers plucked. What a disaster! What a shame? The chickens of glory were exposed and robbed of their feathers...save us children of hen. Where are you my friend, Sahm? Where are the guards?"

Chickens and roosters came from all parts of the farm and gathered those that died either from hunger or torture. Everyone started to talk about safety, security and food.

Where is peace? Where are guards? Where are chiefs?

The white teacher withdrew from them and said, "Please listen to me. The situation is unusual and it seems that things went out of Sahm's control. Sahm will never return while hunger is tearing us apart and killing casting us away. Let's pray and supplicate God to send us the savior quickly and let's ask help from the one who can give it."

"Who can help us? Who can help us?" they all yelled.

"Please listen to me. There are at the hill, farm chickens .They live happily and lavishly. They are capable of feeding us and protecting us from strangers. I don't think they will refuse to help their ancestors," the white teacher said.

" No, no, this is nonsense. You want us to ask help from those artificial chickens! What a shame!" one of the roosters said.

But another said, "Stop being arrogant. I lost my wife and some chicks, so let's the devil help us if he wants to." He kept silent for a while and then said, "I don't mind at all."

Some of them cried, "Woe to you! Where is your pride? White chickens are out of the question. Our master Sahm is coming back."

Tumult overwhelmed the minds of the crowd. Some were asking for help, others were refusing even to think about it. The white teacher sneaked among them with a mean smile. He sat

164

embellishing his beak. He sat far from them observing what was happening.

We are coming to stay, he thought.

25

White chickens were walking in a line to the farms carrying an abundance of supply of food. They started to distribute grains and worms to everyone without exception.

There were few of these who declined the help of artificial chickens. But hunger was unfaithful and the shriek of kids at night was tearing parents' heart apart, so the majority of children of hen accepted them. The attire of dignity and strength became old and then started to wear out here and there, so they resorted to stitch it with threads of humiliation and slavery. Such attire would bring shame to generations to come. But they wished that hard days would be erased by good ones that were coming.

The soul started to shiver on the farm away from the Sahms whom the chief humiliated deliberately with an implicit consent of Haffar who was still convinced that the attire of the savior was made for his matchless veneration.

The number of white chickens was growing faster than many had expected. They would come carrying sometimes food, sometimes medication, sometimes white hens as gifts for prominent roosters. The white guards started to help after the hesitation of the farm residents. The refusal was unanimous if it wasn't for Abu Rish who took personally the responsibility for sending them out once they were no longer needed.

It was an exceptional phase that would be over after the preparation and training of the new teams to work with advanced weapons. Everyone was hoping that these trainings would lead to the punishment of criminals and revelation of the truth.

Who is the killer?

Who's the traitor?

Who and who and who... is manipulating us?

Questions ran from one hen-house to another and from one dunghill to another. The rumors spread in the corners of the farm like plague that a sick chicken would die from infection, while an infected one would die from terror. Promises were increasing day in, day out.

'The truth is coming' was a good word that the two parts were hiding behind until God would fulfill his promise.

Sahm is coming...we will catch traitors... we will expose conspirators... we will find the food stealer...the savior is the solution...the savior will reveal the truth.

Haffar was getting ready for a promising future that he saw from a perspective chosen for him. He took for himself soldiers and guards. Also, the chief and the teacher were preparing missionaries from here and there. They were providing chickens from here and there with food and hatred too. They provided them with goods and sold their conscience, while Haffar was reassured that the crowd was with him because he was really the savior. He became a slave to someone that wanted to take control of everything until God would grant them relief from days of trouble. He was certain that he would reveal the secret and kill the missing hen. He had just to find out who the traitor was, and with the sufficient courage that the teacher and his mysterious world provided him with, he would discover the secret. He would make sacrifices for the sake of the nation. Still, what nation?

The truth became a commodity that was bought, sold, decorated and painted. No one knew what it was, or rather no one wanted the truth to emerge and if you dared to show its head, it would be decapitated. Next, they would have a suitable funeral for it.

The chief arrived in the company of the white teacher and some of his escorts to the dunghill of

168

Abu Rish in daylight giving no heed to anyone. There were two white hens that were imported with them as a gift for Abu Rish who took them happily as he was dreaming of a white hen from the outside of the hill. He accepted them before paying the high price. The chief asked to move to an instant meeting attended by all masters of the farms including Sahm's son.

The teacher stood in front of the audience and said, "I introduce you now to one of the most pious scholars who spent their lifetime in raising the status of all children of hen. He's here to announce the most important news in your life. Here is the chief." He pointed out to him with his wing and said," Go ahead sir. "

The chief took two steps forward and looked at the audience with eyes throwing magical threads like those of a spider. He was setting his trap in the mind of everyone. Everyone had their own thread referred to as friendship between them and the chief and thus he would think he is the chosen.

"With the name of God I start. I greet all of you and thank you for your coming. First, you should know that we were not born cowardly, that we were not born stupid, and that we were not born unable to fly. We were not born cocooned, yielding to other creatures that kill us, eat us and sometimes play with us...and even burn us that our dead body would end in a disgusting stomach or a stinky dunghill.

"That time is over. We are not going to be like that anymore. We had an existence in the past and now we play a big role in refreshing this universe. The story of our lord Nakkar is true. It's not an illusion. I tell you that some of the cravings that were discovered in the dry grottos revealed a lot of truths. The sacrifice of our lord Nakkar would not go with the wind. He started the journey all alone, suffered a lot and became a martyr for us, for me and for you," he said while looking at the crowd as if he talked to every member separately. "We didn't know that until now because the aerial birds hid it. They sent us someone who would suppress truth in us, efface it every day and every moment. They placed that hoopoe called hermit. He is here not only to efface the truth, but also to make sure that you would not learn nor know the necessary talismans to break the spell of the grey-haired witch and Nisr Abu Al-Makhaleb who were the cause of our dire condition. Now, we started to know who we are...realize who we are. The truth is clear; we are no longer stupid. We must be faithful to our lord Nakkar. We must celebrate his memory and follow in his footsteps.

"Let him live inside each one of you. Let us suffer for his absence and loss. Let each one of us suffer for a day in the same way he suffered for our sake for months. And let's be ready to answer his call; his call that he has sent since thousands of years through the carved tablets.

"He said that the savior would come to take us to the place where we are supposed to be. For this reason, we must pray for this savior to be among us in the anniversary of our lord to lead us to the truth. Everyone must know the truth and learn it. The coming week is going to be the memorial of the martyrdom of our lord Nakkar and we will revive his millennium anniversary with dignity and pride. We will tell all creatures the truth; we will break the chain and fly...we were born free and we will remain so. The colored chickens and white ones will be united forever. See you soon in the big meadow at the giant tress."

The audience clapped, slogans rose and wings fluttered.

26

There were hungry chickens and thin chicks that the supply of food which the chief use as bait did not benefit too much. A group of guards was promising this bunch of chickens with the bounties of the chief and a future that no one had ever dreamed of and another was promising them with the return of Sahm, the virtuous and clean-handed leader carrying an astounding truth and a return to serene days.

Days before the celebration, the sacks of grains started to flow into every dunghill whose owner promised to revive the anniversary of our lord and surrendered to the savior. Promises came from here and there, while the crowd's main concern was to silence their stomach growling that increased sadness.

Mothers sold themselves to the devil for the sake of a smile of hope along the beaks of their children that came after a belly full of long-awaited food.

In a nearby place, under the willow tree, the leaves of longing and advice of Nagham and Zaghloul were falling on the head of Sayah. Compassion and tenderness were sagging on him like air making his soul whiter and quenching his thirst for wisdom little by little perhaps it would end up in the store of his memory to explode when needed into streams quenching the thirst of his own kind. His nervousness was immense and the solemnity of the situation was strong.

Shall I take a decision or shall I wait? A few days were separating him from an hour that might be a relief or might be... No, it would be a relief... yes, a relief.

On the night of the commemoration of the so-called anniversary, stunned and scared, Katkout was at the trunk of the old willow, the secret keeper over ages, with his master Sahm. He had just arrived in disguise to tell him about tomorrow.

"It's a bigger day than you could imagine. It's the dream of a big day in the world of chickens."

But Sahm kept looking at him bewildered for though his disguise was funny, his appearance showed misery, and his thin body was the sign of a huge tragedy. His presence today indicated his loyalty and love as well.

"Hi, dear, I have been absent for so long. I missed my loved ones," Sahm said.

"Tomorrow is a monumental day when destiny will be decided. As I have told you before, they will commemorate the anniversary of our lord Nakkar. The white chickens are jostling like flood to the square of the so-called celebration. I'm afraid that colored chickens would end up dull after this painting that the cruel destiny is painting. They are using our beliefs and history. Can you imagine that they are going to have a party for our lord Nakkar and an anniversary commemoration of a rooster that was buried thousands of years ago, while we are groaning under the weight of famine under the name of our lord Nakkar. What are you going to do about this, sir?" Katkout said.

There was no time to answer as a reverent proud big white rooster came out of the nearby bush and said, "Leave him alone, darling. He's helpless and uniformed about the truth. I will tell you what you want."

"Who allowed you to ruin our seclusion?" Sahm said.

"Is this hospitality?" the rooster said.

"Doors must be knocked before entering and meetings' sacredness can't be trespassed unless you are given permission," Sahm said.

"Slow down, Sahm," the intruder said.

"You know my name...so your presence here is not a coincidence," Sahm said.

"Let him go away. Do not panic! I will tell you whatever you want," the guest said.

"Who are you to scare me? And since it is not a coincidence, you then know me well and know that I am not scared of you," Sahm said.

"Forgive me for intruding, but I should come the day before tomorrow," the intruder said.

Sahm said, "So, you're one of the intrusive foreigners. It's okay. Dismiss, dear Katkout, until I call out to you." He said that and looked at the white intruder to hear more.

"Yes, I know you very well though we haven't met each other before. I admired your intelligence because you recognized me. I'm the chief of white chickens coming from the unknown. You know little and I will tell you a lot of things," the intruder said.

"Yes, you're a stranger that came from the unknown and will return to it. Who told you I am looking for information? Aren't we going to meet tomorrow?" Sahm said.

"It seems that you are braver than I thought. Are you going to be there though you are aware of the dangers? Well, you know the news about the commemoration of the anniversary of our lord Nakkar, but you don't know its importance!" the chief said.

"Why are you telling me this now? Do you have any problem? Do you want any help or contribution?" Sahm said.

"I was not intending to tell you, but during yesterday's meeting we decided at Abu Rish's insistence on striking a deal with you to avoid shedding blood and tearing the unity of farms. On behalf of the crowd I flutter in peace so extend for me your wing to create peace between the two sides," the chief said.

"What sides? "Sahm said.

"We and you, our side and yours, your few followers and my many soldiers, my intelligence and your position, white chickens and colored ones," the chief said.

"I don't know the reason for your rudeness to think that you're a partner in my own house," Sahm said.

"There is no time for argument. There is an offer from the group for you and for us including benefits that I think a sage would not miss a chance before fathoming and delving deeply into especially that it doesn't concern you alone, does it?" the chief said.

"A truth that's told with bad intent beats all the lies you can invent. Still, go ahead perhaps the hidden would stop insanity," Sahm said.

"The farms are agitated. Tomorrow is the anniversary of our lord Nakkar and any news can leash hungry souls for revenge," the chief said.

"Did you come here to threaten me or to blackmail me? How rude!!" Sahm replied with firmness.

"Hold on! Put slogans aside. You know that Abu Rush and his power are under our control and hungry chickens whose food you stole will fight you. They are not going to dispose of the one that satiated their hunger," the chief replied.

"Abu Rish is with you! Who are you exactly? Isn't it enough for you that your attempts to famish us were futile?" Sahm said.

Chief: Hold on! I congratulate you on your ability to persevere. But how long can you do that? Your abilities are limited. Can't you see that your own species is hungry? Don't you care about that?

Sahm: Every beat of chickens' hearts has an echo in mine, and the starvation of my own kind is but a simple sacrifice for what they are going to reap tomorrow. As for you, who are you or rather what species are you?"

Chief: It's not a shame to admit that you almost won and that you won that round as I have already mentioned. Still, we have managed to use food as a weapon against you till now. Yesterday, the weapon was dispersed and it might be against you tomorrow. As for our identity, it's a long story.

177

Sahm: Speak the truth, because I know too much.

Chief: We are a bunch of white chickens that were endowed with good without knowing. We were given strength and intelligence beyond your imagination. We have no place where to live or to hide from son of Adam but yours. You wouldn't accept us if we came and asked to settle in your place, and perhaps you wouldn't even believe us.

Sahm: And how would the situation be like between an intelligent chicken and an ordinary one as you claim? How would the situation be like between a hero and a coward, as you say? How would the situation be like between an animal and another that might not be as he thinks? How would there be a harmony? Wouldn't the situation be a ruler and a slave, a superior and a subordinate, a strange scientist and experimental animals?

Chief: No, your interpretation of the situation is wrong. We need you, so that we could ensure stability. We will work together to achieve a real unity. You and Abu Rish would be monumental rulers. We will build for you the most beautiful dunghill. We will support you to have what you want and provide you with the necessary money and comfort. You will have the most beautiful white hens. You and your own kind, or rather our own kind will rejoice over comfort.

Sahm: Where did you get the money to do all this? You only come from a farm where there is neither good nor fortune. You're worse than you think; you want to buy an entire species just to be one of us, to have a homeland. Get out of my sight! Homelands are built not bought.

Chief: You crossed the line that I am running out of my wisdom and patience. Still, suppose what I said is true, what does prevent us from joining you? Give us a chance.

Sahm: You don't know what a homeland means. Homelands are built in the midst of soul land and that of the nation, in the midst of a land that would quench our thirst with its water, while we would satiate it with our blood the day one of them felt the thirst for life, the thirst for freedom and longing for survival. We have been here since eternity and since thousands of years. Every cell in my body and that of every rooster and hen that poked, clucked and crowed at the surface of this earth has an equivalent in a rock or a sand grain or the air breeze. Go away my home is not for sale.

Chief: How arrogant and haughty you are! You are not aware of the size of the risk. Tomorrow is another day, a momentous day for your end and for the beginning of a new era. Tomorrow you might become a rival for your son.

Sahm: Don't worry! I will come to you to take part in the celebration, or rather to share my joy of victory with you.

"What's the use of conquering the universe if you lost your son?" the chief said that and left.

179

A Chapter of the Truth

Big numbers of guards were scattering here and there between the sides of the great plain and farms' entrances. Mottos were on every tree and hen-house and at the top of every dunghill and rock. Sahm's supporters were sharing their mottos though there were many inconveniences that were caused here and there. They didn't accept not to be part of the event. After all, they were the grandchildren of our lord Nakkar. Our lord Nakkar was not restricted to a particular group. He was a great rooster, wasn't he?

There were two teams competing for coming to power. Of course, the audience would not understand unless both good souls and wicked ones allowed them to know. Competitors alone knew what they wanted, while the crowd would follow masters who promised that they would achieve their dreams or they would take them to their aspirations to make money and to rejoice over the leftovers of glory that fell from the comfort trays that were moving in the new glory halls.

The group belonging to Sahm did not explain the story life of our lord Nakkar according to the words of the white chickens and their ally, Abu Rish, but rather considered it a legacy and an icon that imparted a flavor of reverence and a tie to the past.

They felt deep veneration and appreciation for their icon Nakkar. They also wrote and said in the preparation for the occasion, "Our lord Nakkar is everyone's grandfather. Our lord Nakkar is everyone's hero. Our lord Nakkar didn't have any feathery enemies because our enemy is that of our lord Nakkar and his enemy is ours."

However, on the other side of chicken's thinking, our lord Nakkar was the victim who sacrificed himself for the sake of chickens. They pecked the following mottos to excel and to conspire, 'We are all Nakkar', 'Nakkar was the victim of aerial birds', 'Magic will never be an obstacle from now on', and 'I will fly once I break the spell'.

The rumors said that the chief and Abu Rish will give up the traitor to his own kind to avenge on him. They even added that the savior might show up all of a sudden to reveal the truth and unleash it from its long sleep. And perhaps he would break the spell cast upon them.

Stalls here and there were distributing grains and worms along with cold swamp's drink. The white chickens were swallowing their grudge and smiling at everyone. The many supporters of Abu Rish were everywhere observing every single detail. As for the supporters of Sahm, they chose a small slope near the platform according to the instructions of Sahm, the ruler, given by Katkout. Everyone was wondering about the reason for the commemoration of the anniversary of our lord Nakkar for the first time. Next, the explanation prearranged by the chief's clique began. Some of them said that the savior asked Abu Rish to do so; others said that time came to pay tribute to our lord Nakkar.

In the morning word went around that our lord Nakkar was so decent that he couldn't cooperate with witches and that he spent his life in torment as a price for the sake of children of hen, not to mention that he foretold this glorious day as they claimed referring back to his inscriptions in the dry grotto at the sea of darkness.

The goal was to create a fuss and an intellectual emptiness followed by loss and chaos, so that the so-called savior would come and reshape the mob as he pleased, and thus the intellectual crack would be welded carelessly.

The intellectual crack to lead the mob to the edge of the abyss was the goal of every chief aspiring to impose himself as a ruler by force even if he promised that he wanted to be good.

Abu Rish stood on a high dunghill made of dry dung fluttering his wings and waving his tail to the audience. Soon he crowed powerfully announcing the start of the festival. He greeted and praised everyone and complimented our lord Nakkar. He invited the chief to stand next to him and then signaled to him and said, "This noble rooster is the best successor for Nakkar, the Great. Like our lord Nakkar who was generous in his lifetime during the days of grudge and the great conspiracy, the chief risked his life for us in the days of famine and death surrounding us. I won't hide from you that terrorists were on the edge of reaching their goal in these hard days.

"Yes, he risked his life and that of his comrades to bring us food with its different types to save us from a potential death that our enemies conspired against us. He and his own kind rushed to help us carrying arms that they developed to protect their families and themselves. Since they came to our rescue, there have been no longer any casualties or robberies. It's true that we haven't caught the murderer and his accomplices yet, but that was because they retreated under the pressure of the chief and his assistants. Still, we're trying to grab any evidence to chase down the criminals. Our enemy is very intelligent. It seems that his abilities outdo ours. We're in the face of an organized terrorism that wants to destroy us. But we're going to win...win."

Cheers started to rise and rise, "Long live Abu Rish, long live the chief." Abu Rish interrupted them to say, "Today is the day of the truth, the day of our lord Nakkar...it's the day of our lord Nakkar...it's the day of the chief. Let's crow to greet him."

As the crow of roosters rose from here and there, the chief moved forward to take the lead. Abu Rish went on to say, "Here is the white chief who spent his lifetime looking for the identity and the truth of chickens as a whole. Here he is in front of you to warm your hearts with news that would revive shy hope in your chests...he is the master of the truth."

The chief stood with pride and self respect as he was greeting the audience. Chickens were clucking and roosters were crowing. The flutter of his wings was in harmony with chickens ' clucking "truth", "truth", "cluck" ,"cluck".

"My brothers, my ancestors, my friends, today I salute you and salute your hearts throbbing with life. I salute you and salute my brother Nakkar in his grave perhaps he would be happy with the meeting of chickens from his grave. I almost feel that he's blessing our meeting; that great rooster whose life was taken, and who sacrificed his family to keep everyone's dignity.

"The world of aerial birds sold us to Man and took from us the blessing of flying. But we weren't lost and we will never be as long as there is Nakkar in the heart of each one of us.

"Yes, we're late, but we didn't forget. We were sleeping and we woke up. We were stupid and we learned. We were weak and we became strong. Today the words of our lord Nakkar which were found in the dry grotto have become true for the time came when my children who some of them exist; others came into existence killed the common traitor. The talismans of the hoary sorceress were broken and my grandchildren became the masters of space."

"Cluck...the truth...cluck."

Songs were filling the sky. Pride and mischievous victory signs were dancing along the face of the chief.

Where did this damned rooster get this statement from? Abu Rish wondered.

He is really a chief, the teacher thought.

The chief didn't and wouldn't miss this chance for he stood to say, "You learned who betrayed our lord Nakkar because he said it himself. As for me, I will tell you the interpretation of his words about who sold your dreams and himself, but rather the savior would come out now to tell you that himself. Yes, the savior. You all know him. You all saw him. But because of his humility and high decency, he refused to appear in public. Still, the event is stronger than his humility. Greet with me my lord, the savior. He said in a roaring voice followed by a scary silence waiting for the truth storm, so that mercy rain would fall down and the truth sky would be as spotless as yolk."

Opening the curtains of the dunghill began to pave the way for Haffar. The place was overwhelmed with total silence that took them to a slow time period the seconds of which were long days. A silence that was interrupted by a hoarse voice from the top of the tree saying, "Listen to me...believe me for you know me."

Everyone at the tree was surprised and the crowd was stunned for they saw a rooster at the top of it. The rooster was the absent lord Sahm who was pecked by the beaks of sharp-tongued chickens; the master whose glory was sold cheaply in the days of alienation and destitute. His followers shouted the glad tiding, "Katkout was right. The promise he told us is fulfilled."

"Here I came back with the truth, or rather I brought the truth...only the truth; the truth that there is savior in this world. The savior is us, me, you and him... we are all saviors of this beautiful world. If we didn't sell ourselves to these merchants, we wouldn't need a savior. I was never the so-called savior filled with poisons. I, rather, came to liberate you and to liberate myself and my family from the clutches of this wicked clique. This chief is a fake one. He lied, then believed the lie he had told. He robbed our great grandfather of his name to take advantage of your low dreams for his own interests. Abu Rish sold you for his desires, for

186

a blonde chicken and for a red worm to throw you in the sea of misery," Sahm said.

"Anyone who denies the existence of the savior that our lord Nakkar foretold is a liar and lecherous, and Sahm is the one who denied the savior. The one who sold you to birds and stole grains is a traitor, and Sahm sold you and stole your food. Sahm is a traitor and a liar, so don't let him leave. Kill him, kill him... and stand by the side of the savior," the chief yelled.

Haffar rushed toward the platform to say, "I'm the real savior... support me, I support you. I'm the one who will relieve you from traitors and the curse of magic." But the eyes that were looking up didn't take notice of the lowest that's why his untimed talk was in vain; hence, he lost a building whose foundation was a mirage. Abu Rish was stunned by the surprise of the savior before he woke up from the surprise of Sahm who was at the top of a tree he had never dreamed of reaching its lowest branches. He felt that he would be the biggest loser in case one of them won.

He thought and decided that both of them had to lose and to kill each other, so that he would be the biggest winner. So, he looked at Sahm and said, "I know you very well, damned, it's you who communicated with aerial birds and gave them the stocks of supply. You're the traitor, while your son, this brave patriot, is the true savior. He came today just to save us from your evils. You sold your people

187

and traded the teachings of our lord Nakkar for tenets of vice."

Next, he looked at Haffar and said, "If you are the real savior, get rid of your traitor father!!"

Agitation started to rise among the rows of chickens. Talking and posing questions started, "Who shall we believe? Who is telling the truth? Is there a savior or not? We're still famished," said one of the hens.

"We're afraid and terrified," said another.

"There is no safe place to play," the chicks said.

Crowding and jostling started between this team and that team. All of a sudden Abu Rish said to his soldiers, "Kill Sahm. He betrayed his own kind and homeland."

In the meantime, Haffar rushed toward the platform once again, saying, "I'm the savior, I'm the savior."

Sahm was surprised at his son's statement. "We know who you are, son, and you know who we are," Sahm said. "You're not the savior and I'm not a traitor either. We all are seeking a tranquil life."

Here, the chief seized the chance to stir the attendees."Do not play any games," he said. "Don't lie. The truth is that you are a traitor and killing you by your son, the real savior, would impart the blessing of flying to us after he will get rid of the magic knot."

Sahm : Hold on, chickens! How can a rooster like me reach the top of the tree? Yes, how? I must have flown to here. I flew because I found out that the truth lies neither in magic nor in a wizard as this lecherous liar said. It's determination. It's diligent work. As for this white rooster, he's your enemy who came from afar to steal your work and turn you into slaves. They lied to you about the story of the spy bird. They made an honest love story they don't know into a reality of starvation and terror. Tell them, Doctor, about our love story.

The doctor came out of the crowd and said, "It's me who treated her and gave her grains to recover. Sahm was noble for he saved her from the clutches of hunters. Sahm is a great man with a merciful heart. He loved her and she loved him back virtuously and honestly."

Abu Rish sprang up and said, "Stop saying this nonsense. Nothing would do him good because we are going to unite and fly after killing him and killing the secret agents to get rid of the talismans of the damned witch."

The audience screamed, "The truth, the truth, the truth."

Sahm shouted powerfully and confidently, "The truth is that we are so weak and so naive that a group of reckless chickens is taking control of our abilities; the truth is that other creatures called us the underprivileged because we lack determination and we're cowardly; the truth is that our lord Nakkar was neither stupid nor cowardly as these

189

liars claim. Our lord Nakkar was always courageous, but some of his species and allies betrayed him and betrayed our nation that sagged under darkness of thinking and will; therefore, we became known as cowardly and will-less birds.

"Betraying the nation in any era would make a whole country sag under slavery for generations to come, but I promise you that time has changed and the yoke of slavery was broken. There is no turning back. We are not going to let a traitor get away with his treason. We're not going to allow the yoke of intellectual slavery to seize these necks again…we are going to banish the comers from the unknown for goods and will hold the hands of the vulnerable to soar with us in this vast space. Yes, we will soar over all creatures in the vast space and it will always be our supreme goal."

Here the chief shouted, "Liar, liar. He wants to win over your hearts and mercy. He's not the savior. He's a traitor. Where was he in the days of famine? Where was he in the days of terror? It was me who fed you and protected you from murderers. It's me who gave you safety and security."

But Sayah, who fluttered his wings to draw the attention of the attendees, said again, "It's he who started the terror for an inner dirty motive and then stopped it because of a mischievous call from himself. The one who started killing and caused famine is the same one who stopped them. But I'm just here to save you from the snare of dishonesty, hypocrisy, intrigue and false promises. No one will feel fearful or cowardly anymore because we will work hard and energetically. Only with determination and diligent work, we can tell ourselves in front of the world that we are not cowards. Through success and glory we can say that we have a strong will that works tirelessly toward a sublime goal.

"And thanks to God, the hermit and Nagham, I learned that determination and self-knowledge would lead us to the truth, the truth about who we are and where we are heading to. The one who knows the truth would not be disheartened by impurities and obstacles. We will fly high with mind and body. Yes, I can fly and every one of you will by virtue of work, effort and persistence. Through diligent work and devotion, mottos of sorcery would fall; hence, magic and the witch would not exist.

"The truth is that there is Nakkar inside each one of us, there is a leader. Nakkar who dwells in me as he dwells in you pushed me high to the sky with my heart and toward the space with my wings. I'm going to fly in front of you, and every one of you will fly in front of me tomorrow..."

This time Abu Rish stood up and said, "Liar, liar"- he pointed out to Sahm-"I don't know how he reached the top of the tree, but he definitely can't fly."

However, the chief realized the truth that Abu Rish couldn't seize. He was scared that Sahm would fly and the seed of selfishness that he created and planted would die. Therefore, he told his guards, "Kill him. Use your weapons before he would fly and destroy everything we built." But Sahm was resourceful, so he stepped back and flew from the other side as he was saying, "Look, I'm flying." He started to fly and hover over the audience as he was saying, "You all will fly in the air."

The chickens started to shout, "Sahm is flying...a flying rooster, oh my God...we will fly like Sahm...Sahm didn't lie."

The arrows of the chief's clique hit Sahm. He withstood in the space without falling down. What he said and the future of children of hen rested on his endurance. Katkout stood shouting , "O chicken species, O Sahm 's loved ones, O grandchildren of Nakkar, these foreigners are killing your master, your brother, your father... get rid of the white chickens, save yourselves from the clutches of mischief, wash your sins by getting rid of traitors and cowards."

The mob started to clash with strangers who were about to become family a while ago. Soon Sahm was wounded once again. Sahm was hit many times but endured the pain for a long while. In the meantime, the chickens attacked the intruders heedless of the weapons they were carrying.

Haffar stood imploring everyone, "I'm here to save you. Stop that traitor. Find the hoopoe. Find the bird and everyone that helped her and then kill them. It is a big intrigue carried out by the bird and the hoopoe with my father, their secret agent."

No one gave him the slightest attention and many of the supporters of Haffar and Abu Rish started to fight by the side of those of Sahm as the white chickens began to retreat under the commands of the chief. They mingled and the big battle of beaks was launched. Heads were bleeding; crests fell down and blood that was shed left a terrifying impact on chicks learning how to live. Sahm was swaying in the space, while the doctor and Katkout were running to be under him if he fell down as arrows were hitting him from here and there. But the increasing chaos and the withdrawal of white chickens as the chief advised stopped throwing the arrows.

Roosters were fighting. Hens felt cowardly, so they began to run here and there. As for chicks, they were looking admiringly at the flying rooster. Sahm started to revolve in the space falling from high. The hoopoe approached him to support him before hitting the ground, but arrived too late, so he fell down in the course of events.

Abur Rish wanted to withdraw his supporters and run away with the chief to come back later, but they dispersed. Some became loyal to Sahm; others supported Haffar. A few stayed with him. The fight got fierce without knowing what happened to Sahm whom the doctor dragged with the help of

Katkout and Zaghloul to a remote corner to treat him.

The chief withdrew quietly with his roosters and some of Abu Rish's supporters, while Abu Rish took another road as he and the chief apparently agreed. But Sam's supporters did not leave them and hunted them down everywhere. There was no safe place on the hill because all hills were at war. This was hiding behind a rock and another was hiding in a shrub or behind a tree. There was no president or chief running the battle, or rather the battles.

The initiative of individual killing and pecking became the feature of this battle. The scent of blood that was boiling on this ground filled each one of them with a high fighting spirit that no one could realize its essence. Most chickens tried to run away from here and there to the nearest farm to hide with their chicks in their hen-house. But grudge, pressure and suppression were released from unruly roosters and chickens through their beaks, so they took their spite and rancor out on the old and the young.

Blood was running from that face or that crest. Destruction was affecting everything on the farm. The wounded and casualties included chicks, chickens and roosters. Everything was telling each one of them that he was capable of winning through hurting, killing and destroying heedless of the consequences. Everyone killed, or pecked his own kind. Each one of them destroyed a hen-house or ruined a dunghill. But no one remembered that they had a sister or a brother or a mother or a father, so they will show sacredness for others by remembering them. No one remembered the sacredness of their farm to refrain from tarnishing the farms of others.

The battle of beaks continued in the big valley hours and hours... and even for days that everyone was affected by it. Abu Rish and the chief were physically wounded, whereas the destiny of Haffar was unknown. No one survived this battle except for those who escaped and didn't look behind to see what was going on.

The one who leashed their cowardice, survived. They all dispersed. Wasn't it a strange contradiction that the coward survived with the death of the valiant? Only a few days passed until stinky smells reeked of these dead bodies and those incapable of moving. Blood spread like dark spots on green grass thus becoming a source of fetidness inviting nosy hungry noises for a fatty food. Stray dogs started to smell blood scent, fetidness of death and moan of the wounded. Their bark, then, rose intermingling with wolves' howl and foxes' gekkering. The canines of stray dogs had power to resolve matters that the wisest of birds and chiefs could not handle.

Silence reigned in the place and activity became stillness the intensity of which was only broken by the flutter of the wings of Zaghloul that flew to collect life elixir for a body that collapsed.

He would return every day thousand times and perch on a tree trunk that was safe from hungry canines. He would perch with hope tears and the prayer of a powerless soul in his pouch to throw them into the care of Nagham who would mix them with mercy leaves to wipe the wounds of her love that she washed thousands of times with her tears. She was praying and waiting perhaps his heart would beat... and then he would crow.

A whisper of Hope

After many days, on the other side of the world of chickens where some groups of chickens were resting from the hardship of travelling, a young rooster stood looking at the eyes of his hen and said to her, "The chief didn't fly and couldn't, but I saw our lord, Sahm, flying...I see that there is a glimmer of hope to reach the sky. Yes, I will fly like him and carry you high to this sky which is as crystal-clear as a rooster's eye.

The sky was crystal-clear, but the eye of Sahm wasn't, so it closed forever.

Translation of Character Names

- Sahm: arrow
- Awtar: strings
- Sayah: shouter
- Nagham: melody
- Haffar: digger
- Abu Rish: the feathery bird
- Nakkar: pecker
- Abu Kamha: the father of wheat
- Abu Orf: the chicken with crest
- Nisr Abu Al Makhaleb : the clawed eagle
- Katkout: chick

Aeeh PRESS

2021